GRAB
ON TO ME
TIGHTLY
AS IF I KNEW
THE WAY

GRAB ON TO ME TIGHTLY AS IF I KNEW THE WAY

A NOVEL

BRYAN CHARLES

HARPER PERENNIAL

NEW YORK • LONDON • TORONTO • SYDNEY

HARPER ● PERENNIAL

A portion of this novel first appeared in a different form in the *Brooklyn Review.*

P.S.™ is a trademark of HarperCollins Publishers.

HarperCollins books may be purchased for educational, business, or sales promotional use. For information please write: Special Markets Department, HarperCollins Publishers, 10 East 53rd Street, New York, NY 10022.

FIRST EDITION

Designed by Jaime Putorti

Library of Congress Cataloging-in-Publication Data is available upon request.

ISBN-10: 0-06-088298-0
ISBN-13: 978-0-06-088298-3

06 07 08 09 10   ❖/RRD   10 9 8 7 6 5 4 3 2 1

For my mother
and for
Richard VanFulpen

He bent his head forward suddenly, and she drew herself to him in the same moment, her lips half open like a flower.

"Yes," he whispered into her lips. "There's all the time in the world. . . ."

—F. Scott Fitzgerald

**GRAB
ON** TO **ME
TIGHTLY**
AS IF **I KNEW**
THE **WAY**

1

When you grow up you can be anything, they said, but that's a lie too. So I go to band practice and plug in the Twin Reverb, the Stratocaster, and the noise is a beautiful plane crashing into my face. So I make a gun with my finger and thumb and aim heavenward. So I dream of a landscape, this one, darkened by the slow rolling shadows of cloud-sized tits.

2

You can wish in one hand and shit in the other etc. The sun don't shine on the same dog's ass forever etc. I don't know but I been told etc. No matter how much you wiggle and dance the last few drops end up in your pants etc. There is a world war in the heart of every father etc.

3

My name is Vincent Joseph Sweeney and I am an alcoholic. Just kidding about that second part. No one calls me Vincent, or even Vince, except sometimes my mom when she's really pissed. Last Friday I graduated high school. In ten years I'll be dead. That's according to the ninth-grade me, a Jim Morrison disciple. Death at twenty-seven looked good then. Now I say here's to the future, here come the fun times. College, beer, job, marriage, babies, debt, divorce, nuclear annihilation.

4

In the winter we get relentless blizzards, in the summer we get lake-effect humidity that creeps in from the shore and hangs on the air like a wet wool sweater, like now, first heat wave of the year. There's no AC in our house and my parents have their ridiculous cooling method. Around eleven a.m., or earlier some days, they close every window to a crack, draw the blinds and turn on three or four strategically placed fans. I seek relief at the East-Towne 5, a crumbling make-out palace out on Gull Road. Had my first real kiss there. Nora Reperton, beautiful times. Now the East-Towne shows second-run dollar movies and I've been known to see two a day during the hot weather. But no movies today, no nothing. Today I have band practice.

My band is called the Judy Lumpers.

I drive shirtless through the miserable early afternoon, WQXC on the radio *good times and great oldies he digs soul she goes for rock and roll pow! quicksee one-oh-one point nine.* It's stifling, even speeding, with all four windows down, and every song is a comment on the weather.

> *Hot town summer in the city back of my neck feelin*
> *just like a heat wave burnin in my heart*
> *'cause there ain't no cure for the summertime blues.*

Wheeler's driveway is empty. I walk through the garage and into the kitchen, where a girl I've never seen before looks up at me from a book. She's at the small table, bathed in thick hot light and swirling dust and, fuck, I'm shirtless, skinny white chest and three or four long black hairs sprouting from each nipple. Before saying a single word, I run to the car and grab a T-shirt, already damp under the arms by the time I return.

"I'm Vim," I say.

"Helene," she says.

And our conversation ends.

Her face so pale you could touch it and make a ripple, shoulder-length brown hair parted in the middle, green tank top, faded cords, red low-top Converse, great name, great voice. Her eyes so light blue and calm they make me feel like I've been talking too loud my whole life. Down the hall the toilet flushes and a second later Wheeler appears.

Wheeler's been into some shit lately. In the spring he showed up at school wearing a dress and got suspended. He fought back and the next thing you know he's on the front page of the *Kala-mazoo Gazette,* posing in a flowery thrift-store dress on the Gull Lake High School lawn. There's a church about every eight feet here and the Christians went apeshit. Wheeler got called every name in the book by dudes with necks like stacks of tires and even in subtle ways by a couple of the more god-fearing teachers. The controversy blew over but he never returned to school. His dad, the lone parent, tried for a while, made him watch a series of tapes called *Where There's a Will There's an A.* But Wheeler had lost the will. These days he sleeps till noon and designs tattoos, one of which is on his body, an elaborate dragon creature with a tail that goes up his back and curls around his neck.

"Hey Vim," he says, "meet Helene. She's kinda my girl-friend."

His nose is all red and inflamed and I see he's got a nose ring, a gold hoop in the middle, like a bull. "When did you get that?" I say.

"What?"

"The fucking thing in your nose." Why am I suddenly angry?

"This? Yesterday. What do you think?"

Wheeler walks over and Helene puts her arms around his legs and that's when I notice her scars. I lean against the sink and try to see other things but there's only so much to see. A couple minutes pass and I'm just here, stupidly hearing their love whispers, until finally Jake shows up, carrying his bass.

"Thank god," I say.

"What's happening?"

"Just this." I point at the lovers. "Jake, meet Helene."

"Who?"

"Wheeler's kinda girlfriend."

Helene waves. More scars on her forearm.

"Oh no, more than kinda," Wheeler says.

"I'm just going by what you said, Wheeler. You said *kinda*."

"That was then. Now we're full throttle."

"Since when?"

"Since this," snapping his fingers, "right this second."

"No, this second," she says.

"No, this second."

On and on and then they giggle, actually fucking giggle, like we're ten years old and this is recess. I hate these idiotic displays of new love.

"Nice nose, Wheeler," Jake says.

"Thank you. I did it myself."

Then he kisses Helene and the tiny wet smack reverberates like a gunshot. "This is all very great," I say, "but are we practicing?"

THE BASEMENT IS OUR UNIVERSE. Drums, amps and four-track on one end, shredded couch on the other. Almost no light. A lot of the ceiling tiles got busted out the night we had a show here and this repressed minister's son went crazy with his two hours of freedom and pogo'd his head through all of them. There's a single poster on the wall, Marc Bolan coming at you with a Les Paul.

We do our set, then dink around on some new stuff. Jake borrows my guitar and plays a weird dissonant octave chord high up on the neck. Wheeler kicks in with a heavy backbeat. I shrug. "It's okay."

"What do you got?"

"Not much. I'm working on a few things."

"So let's try this."

I sit on the couch and listen for a minute. The song evolves into kind of a Sonic Youth rip, spacy verse bursting into a random, sludgy chorus. It'd be tough to find a vocal pattern for it unless I aped Thurston Moore's awful hipster poetry.

I've got no new songs. I'm trying to get past just ripping off J Mascis but it's tough. Early Judy Lumpers was Dinosaur Jr Jr, me whining in couplets under a three-chord wall of noise with an over-the-top solo at the end. In a way I can't help it. *You're Living All Over Me* is a biblical artifact on a par with *Nevermind* or *Doolittle*. I listened to it so much it went into my bones and blood. And plus I've got the setup for maximum fuzz and volume, the Strat, the '72 Twin Reverb, the Rat pedal, all on permanent loan from my Uncle Bro.

The jam stretches out, Jake and Wheeler fully into it now, nodding at each other before the changes. I get up casually, pretend to look in my guitar case for something, pretend to not find it. Then I go upstairs.

HELENE, STILL AT THE TABLE, STILL READING. I pour a glass of blue Kool-Aid and sit across from her. The kitchen floor vibrates with guitar and drums.

"Hey. Why aren't you playing?" she says.

"Sometimes they get into their thing and I have to take a break."

I look at her arms, the scars, some fat and purple, some thin and almost grayish-looking. My first thought was suicide but now I see that none are on her wrists, which for some reason makes me take them less seriously.

"So what are you reading?"

She holds up the cover. *Naked Lunch*.

Ah the Beat Phase, I'm thinking. Mine came freshman year, when I learned that young Jim Morrison had been a fan of *On the Road*. I smoked a lot of pot in those days, dropped acid in physical science class. I pledged allegiance to the road by occasionally walking home from school. Then my poems, long stream-of-consciousness meditations on sex, death and revolution.

"I read that," I say.

"Yeah I've read it a few times now," she says.

"Wow. There aren't too many books I've read more than once. Maybe *No One Here Gets Out Alive*."

"I read this one pretty much daily." She puts the book down, twirls a lock of hair around her index finger. "It's my bible," she says.

Her what? Bible? Junkies? Anuses, jissom, dripping cunts?

"I feel a religious connection to every page," she says.

"What about every paragraph? I would think that'd be the true test of a spiritual work. If you don't feel a religious connection to every paragraph, you're probably being shortchanged."

"Oh yeah? And what are you probably being, funny?"

My cheeks and neck are instantly aflame. She's silent then, staring with those blue eyes, and the silence is heavy for some reason and I have to keep talking or drown so I say: "I wasn't going for some hilarious zinger, if that's what you mean."

"Well then what were you going for?"

"Maybe just a halfhearted grin, out of pity. Something."

This creates the tiniest of smiles, which I devour. Her face opens up through the curtain of hair in new and beautiful ways. Something is happening here.

"You're not from Gull Lake."

"No, I go to Loy Norrix."

"So how do you know what's his name?" I point at the floor.

"You mean Bixby? We met at the park."

She means Bronson Park, downtown Kalamazoo, where the punks, skaters and rejects from all the different schools in the area commune. You see them in droves, after school or on weekends, doing railslides in the parking lot or sprawled on the lawns in stoned, angry heaps.

I lean in and stare down her scars, no shame, like if I just stare long enough they'll open like little mouths and say how they got there.

Scars with voices telling their funny tales of mutilation.

Please baby, tell me what happened.

Let our scars have a conversation.

The basement jam drones on. I take a thousand baby sips of Kool-Aid just to have something to do. Helene looks back at her "bible." I look too. There's writing in the margins, whole passages starred and underlined, a note in large print across the top of pages 156 and 157. *I Was Just Saying I Love You. Not Saying Any Longer. I Am.*

The heat is unreal, like the heat of all summers forever in this one room. Thinking makes me sweat. Skin like flypaper. Looking at Helene makes me sweat.

I see a drop of sweat at the top of her cleavage and wait for it to drip.

If it won't drip, if it won't fall, I'll walk out in the yard and throw rocks at my heart. I'll fucking get in my car and smash into a tree.

And god must really care, even though he doesn't exist, because the drop falls, it disappears between the tits, and a door in my mind kicks open so loud it almost makes a sound in the real world.

She glances up, catches me staring, and smiles.

And just like that I'm saying her name over and over and dreaming of stealing a kiss, a quick one, and the inside of my head is all painted with visions. Helene and I ascend through clouds into atheist heaven on a water bed with angel wings.

5

Now I want everyone. The counter girl, I want her too. She's got the uniform. How I love a gal in uniform. Polyester on ass, the black, orthopedic-looking shoes, the tight button-up with stripes and a name tag. *Teena*. Teena peeks up from under her visor. She's maybe five feet tall or less. Yes Teena, climb me like a redwood, commence humping. She slides the tray over. Two Whoppers and a cup for water.

6

I'm sitting in my car, an '83 Subaru hatchback handed down from my mother, in the Gull Lake Café parking lot. The Café is the semi-fancy restaurant of the area and I've been here since day one, before day one, hired when they were still putting up drywall. My application at the time had said busboy—like MLK, I had a dream—but I balked when they asked if I'd mind cutting my hair—it was over the ears then, sort of Peter Buck or *Rubber Soul* Beatles—and that's how I began my career as a dishwasher.

It's dead this time of day, mid-afternoon, just a few staff cars in the parking lot and the dumpsters way in the far corner. I've got the black-and-white checkered kitchen pants on, still stinking and greasy from last summer.

I'm ready for warfare.

On the other side of the Café and across D Avenue is the southern end of Gull Lake itself. I look at the dashboard clock. In five minutes I'll be late for work.

I leave the car and walk down to the bay, onto the public dock, out among the lake people and their screaming tans. Behind me is the Gull Lake Market, to my left is the Filling Station, the place for burgers and ice cream. Both doors have leather strips of bells that jingle infinitely.

The day is pure blueness, all sky and water.

I turn around and see Dale the Hippie ahead. Dale and I started on dish together, hired the same day, but he stayed on after I left that fall, the fall of Desert Shield, and he's been there ever since. "Vim Sweeney," he says with slow stoner voice. He's leaning against a mountain bike, holding a mini thing of orange juice, long blond hair vaguely wet or greasy.

"Say there, Dale. What's the good word?"

"Hydroponic."

"Do go on."

"Skip tells me you called him up, signed on for another tour."

Skip is my boss, head chef and co-owner of the Café.

"That's true. I'm on my way there now."

"Ouch. I'm off today. Takin a little ride. One end of the lake to the other. Plus check it," pulling down both eyelids, "I'm completely baked."

Dale is one of those guys who can get high and function perfectly in the world, talk to the cops, give a deposition, do the alphabet backward, whatever.

"Still a dish dog?" he says.

I nod and look away. He's wearing only thumbnail-sized Umbros, a pair of Tevas and a fanny pack for his pot materials.

"You maybe heard I'm a salad boy now."

"Sure, who hasn't? It's all over Reuters and CNN."

"You're a funny guy, Sweeney, I like you. That's why I'm going to kill you last."

"Still taking classes?"

"The U of L, duder. University of Life. It's a big old shitty school."

"I applied there," I say. "Didn't get in."

"I'm . . . fuck," he says, "I'm hungry."

"So go eat."

"Eatin's for pussies." He flashes the old thumbs-up and then pedals away.

7

It's like a time warp in the kitchen, not one thing has changed. I think even the same CD is playing as when I walked out the door last fall. Squeeze, *Singles 45's and Under*. Skip seems fatter but still has the goatee, still has the back part of his hair pulled into a ridiculous microscopic ponytail. "Let's get you started on okra," he says.

The other dishwasher shows up. Wendell. He looks about forty, half a dusty beard glued onto a leathery pockmarked face. Skip has him do okra and puts me in the walk-in, where I fill champagne glasses with white chocolate mousse, fill my mouth too, straight from the squeezer. Soon I'm on a sugar high and my head feels full of gas.

Life in the cooler reminds me of a dream I had many years before Desert Storm. My sixth-grade class is kidnapped and stuffed in a meat locker. Every half hour a guy with a ski mask takes one of the kids out and shoots them in the head. We hear muffled gunshots through the airtight metal doors. Then me. I'm the last one left and I get it too. They say you can't die in your dreams but I did. My blown-out brains grew eyes.

Skip opens the door just as I've swallowed a huge mouthful of mousse.

"Turn and burn, Vim," he says, dumb code for the dinner rush.

I leave the cooler, get punched by the heat. The line sizzles and smokes, the cooks speak their chatter. Someone shouts an order for the veal. I walk to the Hobart and the rest of the kitchen disappears behind the glass racks.

Water, wine, coffee cups.

"You wanna wash, you want me to wash?" Wendell says. He's a little guy, wiry, with a faded Rolling Stones tongue tattoo on his bicep.

"What do you prefer?"

"Don't even matter. Your choice." A little of his breath sneaks out, pure smoke.

"I'll wash."

"All right, good enough." He fills the three metal sinks behind us—wash, rinse, sanitize—and we wait.

A busboy appears, from this vantage just tanned arms emptying a tub. He puts the glasses in the racks and the excess water rains onto my shoulders. Then the splashes of wine. He scoots over the pile and so it begins. Open the Hobart, steam pours out and blinds me, slide in the rack, close the Hobart, wait ninety seconds, repeat till you're dead. Ashtrays, ramekins, steak knives, creamers. Wendell weaves through the kitchen traffic, plates stacked chest-high, almost graceful in his big puffy Nikes and ripped jeans. My arms are slick and shiny with grease, my palms and fingers shriveled white like a bloated long-dead corpse, my T-shirt, apron and crotch are soaked, I'm made of sweat and steam.

"Behind!"

"Hot pan!"

"Behind!"

"Hot pan!"

And the pan hits the air hits the water with a hiss.

Wash, rinse, sanitize, wait.

Now I'm salivating over bus tub scraps like a dog that can't tell the difference between love and a beating. I eat a chunk of burger, some steak fat, a few soggy fries, a hardened roll, a crust of a piece of peanut butter pie.

Wendell doesn't talk. He sings Van Halen under his breath, sings *could this be magic or could this be love? Could this turn tragic? You know that magic often does.*

I wonder if I'll ever have a job that doesn't feel like someone richer than me is stealing my life and punching my spine every second.

I see lonely ships upon the water.

8

The house is quiet when I walk in, it seems untouched for many years. The drone of crickets in the swamp out back, low burp of frogs, the fireflies like Christmas lights in the darkness. The air is cool and sweet and seeps through the screen like a drug, an anesthetic. I turn on Letterman. I'm happy now, I'm dull.

9

And I would like, since you asked, to crack the world in two and fuck its blistering molten core. It's true, I've never fucked, but it's also true that I see angels drowning in the strange dark places between dreaming and waking and going insane. I don't mean literally I mean figuratively I mean open your eyes, Vim. You're at the Crossroads Mall, wandering the food court. Grab a Hot Sam, an Orange Julius, some Boardwalk fries. Get in the photo booth, pull the red curtain, put in your dollars. Four quick flashes and wait. The strip comes out and surprise! You're still your same dipshit self.

10

My mother is in the kitchen drinking a glass of red wine, heating leftover spaghetti. I'm at the counter, deep in a can of honey roast peanuts. A little red radio tuned to NPR blares *All Things Considered*. She's news-obsessed, so much so the TV in the living room is also on, tuned to channel three, CBS local and then Dan Rather.

All the different voices collide into static.

And there's Ed, my stepdad, in his big blue recliner, desperate to change the channel, flick around for a hunting or fishing show, a John Wayne movie, QVC, anything. I know because her news fetish has been their joke going on however many years. Another long-running joke turned real life. He appears in the doorway, white T-shirt tucked into blue jeans, one of maybe three outfits I've ever seen him wear. Ed's an electrician and pipe fitter at Pearl Paper, works every day of the year, including Sundays and some major holidays. He cocks his head toward the radio and says, "Great, more news. Welp. Long as I'm up." He opens the fridge and takes out a beer.

"Right on," I say. "Miller Time. Hand me one of those, willya sport?"

"Sure you can handle it? First beer's always a killer."

"That's what I need, man, a killer. Something to kill the pain."

"Pain of what?" He pops the top and takes a big old swig. "Dishpan hands?"

11

It's all in the papers about this Kalamazoo kid who signed to the New York Yankees for some absurd amount of money. I've never heard of the guy, but he's my age, my grade. He graduated high school three weeks ago, like me, and is now a beloved millionaire, unlike me. Everyone they interview, all his friends and teachers, they all say the same thing, what a nice guy, how smart and polite, how destined for greatness.

Plus the time I ran into this girl, a friend of a friend I was trying to make time with, and she couldn't shut her face about it.

"Hey, did you hear about Derek Jeter?"

"No, who?"

She told me everything I already knew from the paper and TV, like he's so rich and great etc. "It's exciting," she said, "it's weird, I mean I slow danced with him."

You could see her practically fucking the memory.

"He asked me out a couple times," she said.

"Dynamite, wow, first-rate."

"You know, it's true what they say. . . ."

But I didn't hear the rest because I was walking away.

I won a poetry contest once. Two contests, really, but the same poem both times. Yet where is the fawning snapper? Last fall the Judy Lumpers sold out Dick's Basement, the little rock club in Quincy. We made $200 playing ten songs, all originals, no covers. Yet where are my profiles on News 3 and in the *Kalamazoo Gazette*?

Where are the prophecies of my greatness?

12

Another band practice. Helene is here but nearly mute, sitting on the couch in the basement, writing nonstop in a spiral notebook, *Naked Lunch* on the next cushion. The way the mic is set, I have to face her, but she doesn't look up, not for a second, not even at Wheeler. It's all just this furious writing.

At the break, Jake and I sit in the backyard and pass a bottle of piss-yellow Gatorade. I lie back in the grass, hear a lawn mower, kid laughter, pool sounds, a phone ringing in Wheeler's or the next house, a woman's voice, *Jessica no honey no that's your brother's.* I smell fresh-cut grass, laundry from the dryer vents, my own BO.

A diving board bends and releases, a body comes down into water.

Trevor honey be careful I said.

"So we see the way you're looking at this girl," Jake says.

"We? Who's we?"

"Me."

"We is me?"

"*Oui, oui.* Like a fuckin French porno."

"I do love the Frogs."

"Which reminds me. Ya know what FROG stands for?"

"What?"

"Former Republic of Germany."

"Brilliant."

"You like that one. Shit, I knew ya would. Heard that one on Parris Island, my bunkmate there, big fella name of Jasper, big dumb sumbitch. Man, I got a million more too. Old Jasper he used to could never shut up."

"Okay so wait so picture this."

"Yes?"

"A man walks into a wax museum."

"Heard it."

"Priest, rabbi, rowboat."

"Yeah and by the way what's up with airplane food?"

"Thanks a lot, you guys have been great, I'll be here all week."

"So vee see ze vay you look at ze Fraulein."

Back downstairs I turn the mic away from Helene and we do our set a second time: "Built Myself But I Exploded," "Gulf War Lover," "Moons Over My Hammy," "Isn't It Pretty to Think So," "Last of the Hell Driver's Club," "Presumed Debutante," "Stay Cool Forever," "Otto Loves Esme," "All the Young Hessians," "Fuck Me in the Year 2000," "Slouching Towards Kalamazoo."

> *I watch some kids, they radiate*
> *All the symptoms I once had to fake*
> *Shot from the barrel of goodwill*
> *To coalesce inside the morning din*
> *Draw me a picture when you're high*
> *Because it's too late, I'm so great*
> *I tried to break your heart in a nice way*
> *The stars and the streetlamps*
> *Ignite the sterile suburbs.*

Jake walks by as I'm turning off my amp.
"Vee see you," he says.

13

Music, I remember my mother gave me music too. I remember those records, real records with the pop and hiss and the dust jackets fanned on the living room floor. She would listen every endless Saturday afternoon, the same records week after week.

Simon and Garfunkel, Janis Joplin, Don McLean.

And to me all the songs sounded like fall, like things ending, leaves blowing over dead grass, the cold ground, Leonard Cohen's voice hollowed out by hope and despair singing *like a bird on the wire like a drunk in a midnight choir I have tried in my way to be free.*

When I heard this a great scream bloomed inside me.

14

There was a soundtrack to this, Joe Jackson *Look Sharp!,* but the CD skipped and someone said *Fuck* and it stopped. Now there is only the music in my head, little fragments, the best parts—a chord change or lyric—of all the songs I wish I'd written.

I got no lips I got no tongue where there were eyes there's only space.

Time frozen like Gull Lake in January, all the hands blown off the clocks.

I load another rack and run it through and when it comes out Wendell says, "Come on, Sweeney. You been runnin shit racks, dude. This one's half empty."

"We can't all be winners, Wendell."

"Say what?"

"I said they can't all be winners."

Sizzle and hiss, smoke and oil, sauté pans scrape the burners.

"No I know but they said they wanted it medium well."

"Go tell em ask em what the fuck they think this is."

"Skip I know I'm sorry but."

"Fine just fuckin set it there for now, turn and burn, Dougie, drop some fries."

Behind hot pan order in order hot pan behind.

"How we doin on that chicken pot pie?"

"Hey fellas hey there we need forks you guys just whenever you guys get a chance." Another stack of plates moves toward me and another and another. The top plate has a half a piece of cold lasagna, grease congealed in the pockets of cheese. I peel off the first two layers, tilt my head back, swallow whole, like a snake on a nature show eating a goat.

"Hey Sweeney, man, share the wealth."

Wendell eats the rest in a sandwich made with two limp lettuce leaves. He smears his fingers around a dessert plate and licks off the raspberry sauce.

"Gimme a New York strip medium gimme a chick Caesar gimme a burger medium bacon and cheddar gimme a JERK! Ha, hear that, boys, gimme a JERK!"

Skip does this every time someone orders jerk chicken, shouts it like it's a brand-new gag and we all should fall down laughing. There should be a statute of limitations on jokes. Skip gets a week for the jerk chicken thing and then by law has to come up with new material. Letterman, you're a god but come on, enough about Saddam Hussein or New York cabdrivers or whatever the fuck it is.

Plus the joke that is everyone's life.

What were Vim Sweeney's last words?

What's this button for?
Where'd he take his vacation?
All over Florida.

THE LAST THING LEFT IS TO SWEEP and mop but right now Wendell and I are sitting on the edge of a boxed-in plot of dirt Skip set aside for an herb garden but which sprouts only a few sad weeds. Wendell smokes and hacks up phlegm and launches goobers into the parking lot. I am eating the fingertips of my left hand, guitar calluses broken open by steam and water. Dale the Hippie comes out, hair up under an old Tigers cap, apron untied and stained red at the waist. He lights a cigarette. "That's right, men. Look alive."

Wendell expectorates.

It's a hot night but breezy, less humid. Across the street and up the hill from the Café is the Bayview Gardens, with a big fake ship, a giant wooden monstrosity, on the lawn out front next to a sign that says who the entertainment is—sometimes it's the Dream Police, my Uncle Bro's band—and what the specials are and occasionally has cute or inspiring sayings. *THIS WEEKEND PETE MURDER BAND NECESSITY IS THE MOTHER OF INVENTION.* The band's still playing and "Mustang Sally" drifts through the back door out over our heads. Dale cups his ear away from the noise. "I think I hear Denver calling," he says.

"What's in Denver?" says Wendell.

"Nothing, everything. Hunter S. Thompson, the mountains."

Song ends. Cheers and applause. *All right everyone all right it's surely late but Pete Murder's only just gettin warmed up here, we're only just gettin started. This next one's a bit of a rattlesnake so you know what to do just grab your lady or grab your man and why don't y'all just walk. This. Way.* Cheers and applause. The opening drumbeat, the lick.

"Fuck Denver," says Wendell.

"Why, you ever been out there?"

"Nope, you?"

Dale pauses. "No."

Wendell goes on, "Trust me, bro, you don't gotta visit a place to know you don't dig it." He flicks his cigarette and it hits the pavement in a burst of sparks. "I mean, if I had a dollar for all the things I thought would suck and they ended up sucking, well, I'd be shittin in some pretty tall cotton."

So I took a big chance at the high school dance with a missy who was ready to play. Wasn't me she was foolin 'cause she knew what she was doin when she told me how to.

"Yes sir, if it's one thing I know, one place is the same as the next. Don't matter where in the world you live, you still just eat, shit, work and die."

"Eat shit?" I say.

"Yeah that too," he laughs.

"Where you from, Wendell?"

"Man, that's a good question. I feel like I just kinda . . . showed up one day."

"No for real."

"I'm bein for real."

"No seriously."

Putting a hand on my shoulder he grins. "And I'm serious, Sweeney, I thought you said you finished high school, bro, because if you did you'd know I came screamin out my mama's pussy, same as you. Same as everyone."

15

I drive with the windows down without music so I won't disturb the night, stop to let a deer cross 37th Street. We are the only creatures awake or alive. Except there's another one standing frozen in the woods to the left of the road, reflector eyes staring out.

The darkness is immense and the sound of it.

I take a long shower and walk through the house. Outside my parents' room I linger and listen. The ceiling fan hums and squeaks. Ed has a deep bass snore, so loud he sometimes wakes himself. My mom breathes an endless series of little gasps, as if afraid of all she's seeing down in her dreams.

Tell her I love her telepathically, how else?

If I could write just one song with the feeling of hearing my mother sleep.

Go in your room and lie down.

Helene.

Her voice an echo ringing back, last thing you hear before sleep hits, her hair a shroud to bury or burn you in, beneath her shirt is a heaven of creamies like nothing you've known. You see her in black bra and panties bent way over and everything then is fear and desire. You sidle up and touch and melt.

16

What about you, dad? Flip you. No dad, what about you? Flip you. Etc. See I don't think I need to sit with you freakin dummies anymore.

A woman in a fake living room with blinding white carpet. Oops, there goes the glass of red wine. A look of horror. Guy comes in with a little tube of something, squirts it on the stain, the stain vanishes. But wait, there's more. Now he's in a fake kitchen, standing at an island counter with a big bowl of water. Guy holds up a jar of black ink, watch this. Dumps in the ink. Prepare to be amazed, holding up the tube, one drop is all it takes. Squeezes in a drop. And the really great thing? It is absolutely one hundred percent safe. And to prove it. Sticks his hand in the water, swishes it around, water goes from black to murky to clear. Act now and get.

A comedy about.

And I was like. And he was like. So I was like.

Do you think your name will be on that plaque? Yes sir. That's pretty arrogant considering the company you're in. Yes sir. I like that. The uh plaque for the alternates is in the ladies' room. Oh you kill me you really do.

I was like whatever I was like.

A brutal murder, a brilliant killer, a cop who can't resist the danger.

The pep rally's gone out of control and here we are now, the final shocking scenes, the mouth, the stubble, the scream. A denial a denial a denial.

A comedy about what happens when.

I'm a smellologist and this smells good.

I shall not seek and I will not accept.

But wait, there's more.

Are you ready to rock? Are you ready to party?

17

Once upon a time Gruber Dills was the guy who roamed the halls endlessly with Birks flopping and a smirk on his face while everyone else sat in class. A senior when I was a freshman, dealer of low-rent drugs, including at one point caffeine tablets. When busted with said tablets by school authorities he used as his defense the fact that the cafeteria was fully stocked with pop machines. Voted Male Worst Driver Class of '89. Now a resident of Kalamazoo's student ghetto and day manager at the Big Burrito, where he serves me a baja chicken combo meal and tells me all about the Big Fuck You.

"Landlord's kicking us out," he says, "got us on some bullshit trumped-up charges. Tonight's our last night in the house. It's gonna be decadence, Sweeney. Filth and decadence."

"Don't forget I had extra guacamole." For some reason there's a tip jar by the register. I put my bills away, make a show of dropping in a few stray coins. "Filth, you say?"

"Real rock-bottom shit."

"Well I do enjoy a big fuck you."

"824 Vine Street," he says.

FIRST THING I HEAR walking down Davis is the bass line to "The Joker," so faint it could be a dream or a memory. The WMU practice field is on my right, locked and empty in the metallic dusk. On the hill behind that is East Hall, part of the old main campus. Looks like an antebellum mansion up there, lights blazing around broad white columns. Take a left on Vine and "The Joker" gets louder. 824 is set back from the street, down a narrow driveway, among the shrubs and neighboring yards. Bodies in the front window, bodies on a plaid couch on the porch, every mouth breathes smoke, every hand holds a drink. The steps sag beneath my feet.

"Welcome, friend," says one of the couch guys, "do you like to party?"

"Sure. Gruber sent me."

"So he did. Five dollars, please."

"For what?"

"We've got a full bar inside, friend. This is an all-you-can-drink affair."

He takes my cash and with a black Sharpie writes on the back of my hand **Fuk U**.

Then I'm inside, in the living room.

Heat and smoke and beer and sweat, a haze in the air over everyone's head. There's a table with a stereo and huge speakers and a guy behind it, rifling through piles of CDs. One wall has a poster of Robert De Niro with a mohawk and shoulder holster, another has Pearl Jam with swastikas drawn on their foreheads. I scan the crowd for someone I know and find no one.

In the back, in I guess the dining room, is the bar.

Now I've got a red plastic cup spilling over with Bell's Amber Ale, lick my knuckles, now it's gone, get back in line. Gruber Dills emerges from the crowd.

"Hey Gruber. I like what you've done to the place."

"There he is. There's my man. Here's my dude right here." Gruber's face is flushed and glistening. His T-shirt is soaked. His eyes swim in ten directions.

"You had this shit yet?" He breaks the safety seal on a bottle of Robitussin and sucks it down in three big gulps.

"How is that? Refreshing?"

"Like this," he says and moves the bottle slowly across his forehead like a guy in a Budweiser commercial. "Like I wanna fall backwards into the fucking pool." He pitches it over his shoulder. A phantom hand pulls him back into the mass.

Gone but I still hear his laughter.

"Another amber," I say.

A minute later I say the same thing.

I AM DRINKING AND STARING and that is all. This is like a movie party, like a beautiful cyborg woman could bust through the door any second and make the nerds and jocks dance together. The Beatles are on but it's fucking Ringo's voice, "With a Little Help From My Friends," and everyone sings the chorus so they can shout the word *high*. What's next, the Dylan song that goes everybody must get stoned?

Come on, if it's got to be classic rock, play the White

Album, "Yer Blues" or "Helter Skelter." Or "The Soft Parade," by the Doors. Get a little death out.

I'm losing track of something.

Vim Sweeney stands in the room with the noise. Don't be like this, he thinks. But he's tired of growing out of things. Tired of coolness. Tired of the questions that plague his idiot brain, like what next what now what exactly do you want?

Well. I wanna kiss wet arms, wanna lick sweat for nourishment, wanna clutch the smell of perfume in my hands and throw it at the sky and make a new atmosphere. Or hairspray or peach hand lotion. Or lip gloss even, grape lip gloss with sparkles in it. Let me have a little something. Throw me a bone. It can't all be dreams. It can't all be—death to this word but—*yearning*.

Take another sip.

I'm thinking about things.

I picture half these people wearing ties in offices five years from now.

YOU'VE GOT ANOTHER BELL'S and the light from dead stars traveling into your toes. Out back, in the tiny yard, the night opens up like the blackness from before you were born.

But the moon but the glowing gray clouds but the breeze in your hair.

You're drinking and listening and nothing else.

Voices jump out of the air.

"I read those. Of course. Read the whole series," she says.

"I remember I read one, just to see. Big secret at the time. Read the one with the twins," he says.

"Are you crazy? They all had the twins."

"Okay. Shit. The name. I remember the name. *Double Trouble,* it was called."

"The very first one."

"So I read the very first one."

"Why the hell?"

"Just to see."

"And I'm out on the lawn," he says, "looking in the dirt for some fucking pebbles or something."

"Pebbles?" he says.

"Something, you know, to throw at her window and get her attention, but there's no pebbles. Now what lawn, what piece of earth, doesn't have pebbles?"

"I don't know but that word. Stop saying it."

"So I've got this rose in my hand and she's up in her room and it's romantic and perfect except there's no pebbles."

"Stop saying pebbles."

"Not one."

"Her boyfriend's a marine," she says, "not even cute."

"Face like a fetus in a jar," from the other chick.

"I guess he was in like Desert Shield."

"But what I do have, I've got all this change," he says, "this pocketful of change. So I'm throwing coins at her window and the pennies aren't cutting it and the dimes are like bouncing off into the grass. So, last resort, I'm flinging quarters and pretty soon I'm out like two, three dollars, more than the cost of the shitass rose, and I'm all out of breath on the fucking lawn alone all for a chick who."

"Wait," you say, coming out of yourself now, "hold on."

"Hi," she says.

"Hey," she says.

You remember watching Letterman the night of your sixteenth birthday, tired beyond tired, your body empty of blood and heart. We interrupt this program. Tom Brokaw comes on, says Iraq has invaded Kuwait and whatever whatever. Who gives a fuck? you said. You wanted Dave back and only got scared later, when there were like bombs and shit. A black screen, bright flash and that was it, the whole fucking war.

"Desert Shield or Desert Storm?" you say.

"Desert what?"

"The fetus face, was he in Desert Shield or was he in Desert Storm?"

"What's the difference?"

"Oh stop it," shaking your head, "just stop that talk."

THE KITCHEN WINDOWS ARE STEAMED. The floor is slick and streaked with dirt. The counters are a fallout of plastic cups and half-eaten food and empty bottles. The sink is filled with water and floating cigarette butts. The overhead light flickers like a vague idea. I'm still a stranger and loving it. Then a hand on my shoulder.

Jake says: "What is best in life?"

I say: "To crush your enemies, see them driven before you, and to hear the lamentation of the women."

"I saw your car all the way down Davis. How long have you been here?"

"Not long."

"Seen anyone else?"

"No, you?"

"No. I talked to Wheeler. He said he was coming but I don't see him."

"What's that you're drinking?"

"A white Russian. Try it."

"Jesus, that's delicious. Tastes like fucking cereal."

"I always thought melted ice cream."

"I want one."

"Let's go back to the bar."

The room slants and the walls sigh. A guy and a girl draw on each other with markers. Bono sings "Red Hill Mining Town." The bartender leans toward me.

"Can I get a white Russian but can I get it in this?"

"The fuck is that?" Jake says.

"It's a thermos."

"Where'd you get a thermos?"

"Kitchen cupboard."

"Well," the bartender says, staring at the thermos. "All right. I mean, what the hell, right?" He pours in the stuff, shakes it up and hands it over.

"Look," I say, "the best part. I can drink out of the cup that screws on top."

"To rock," Jake says, raising his drink.

"And to roll."

OR ELSE HERE'S TO THE FUTURE, what this is supposed to be. Or else say it. You don't know how. You're becoming a creature in one of the upstairs bedrooms. The other faces burn with a heightened clarity and what the fuck are you talking about now?

"Happens all the time," you say. "Sign these contracts. Just fucking kids. Got their dream out there like a dream on a stick."

"Like a carrot, you mean?"

"Carrot, fucking carrot, whatever. Kid signs, what happens? Chuck him in the farm system, class A ball, make him a fucking slave. Ever seen *Bull Durham*?"

"Is that the one with uh?"

"Early Costner."

"Fucking Costner."

"I liked him in uh shit. It was a western uh *Silverado*."

"Yeah but fucking *Robin Hood*?"

"I liked uh what was it, *Fandango,* sort of a road movie and he's."

"Buttfucking Robin Hood."

"What's in the thermos?"

"So he works his way to triple A, so what? Nothing but the third level of hell, different kind of torture. Trust me, Jeter's gonna play in the bush leagues for twenty years, till he's old and useless, then the Yankees force him under contract to be a talent scout. He's the old guy sitting in the high school bleachers with a case of Pepto-Bismol and a bottle of Wild Turkey to kill the pain of his obliterated dreams. It's exciting now but trust me baby you will never hear the name Derek Jeter again."

"You think?"

"Baby I *know*."

ALL THE T-SHIRTS ARE COMMERCIALS, all these pricks have second sight, will you please open your books to page fuck off.

Isn't anything.

Life is easy.

I touch my nose in the reflection.

What the fuck does anybody want?

I want to find someone to love who loves me back then ball her till her voice becomes a sun ray. I want to eat my own heart and shit out music. I want to save the lives of all my friends and smash the heads of my enemies. I want to pull my mom out of time. I want to want something more than two weeks' vacation and ten sequels to *Wayne's World* and a new kind of pizza with cheese stuffed in the cheese.

Pounding on the bathroom door.

"Buddy, you better be dying for how long you're taking."

"Me? No. I'm alive. I could stay here forever."

"Please don't."

"Wow. I can't believe this is really my face."

"It is. Now come out of there and let me do my thing."

"Gimme a minute."

"Please, buddy, this is a grade-A fuckin emergency."

Ed's voice comes into my head like a remembered dream. *You can wish in one hand and shit in the other and see which one fills up fastest.*

"Fuckin bathroom'll smell like Auschwitz when I'm done."

I lean my forehead against the door. "I'm coming out now."

"Buddy, for the love of god."

I've got my hand on the lock. There's a good time out there or someone's idea of one. All I have to do is open the door.

JAKE AND I PASS ON THE STAIRS. He says, "Hit me."

I refill his cup.

He says, "Hit me again."
The thermos is empty.

THE PEARL JAM POSTER'S GONE. Two fist-sized holes in the plaster. One of the walls looks sprayed with blood. There are people dancing, woo-hooing, and the living room floor shakes, it thunders, and every window's open, ceiling fan full blast but it's not enough to carry away the sour smell of alcohol sweat that seeps from our skin like a gas.

I need this, need to be in there, writhing colliding with the young men and women that's how I see them down a long tunnel of age looking up from my grave through the hollows of the eyes of my corpse.

Hit me. Hit me again.

I need everyone now, all the love and titties or hey a fist in my face or an elbow to the chin foot in the gut hot iron on the balls hey smash me I turn beautiful turn a thousand shades of green the color of my eyes color of my father's eyes color of the place in my head where desire is a symptom of disease.

Fuck your head, Jack. Let's dance.

The DJ's on some '80s kick. "Our House," then "Come On, Eileen." I come alive inside the song, throw my body around the room, against the walls and pushed-away furniture. I pull down Travis Bickle, tear him to shreds, throw him up like confetti. All the years of no dancing have turned me into this discarded toy.

Hey ladies, are you ready for, well, nothing?

No life or dream of life will ever be good enough.

Here comes the breakdown, the slow shuffle, and what's this what the fuck, two hands slip into mine. Here's Wheeler and Helene.

Flames lick the corners of my vision.

We dance, the three of us, in a tight spastic circle as the song builds back up. Wheeler is shirtless, shrieking a kind of scat, wallet chain swinging from his cutoff camouflage pants. Helene's face is gone in her hair but I see the rest, mutilated arms and even her legs. A skirt? She didn't seem the type.

Somewhere—I'm airborne at the time, trying to take them with me—a light goes out, shatters or whatever, and the living room darkens. Wheeler spins away, breaks our chain, pogos off through the crowd. I grab Helene's free hand and pull her closer and the room sings the room sings the room sings.

Come on, Eileen, ohhhoh something some-thing. At this moment. You mean everything.

Holding her like the song is the sea and she's the life raft I'm sinking away from. But it fades, it ends, it has to. Helene lets go as "Down Under" kicks in. She shakes her hair back licks her lips her right hand touching her throat.

Is the planet trembling or only my heart?

"Hey," she says.

"What?"

"I said hey. H-e-y."

Wheeler returns with his beautiful smile. "That was killer," he says.

I'm trying to remember to breathe.

He reaches for my hand, for her hand. "Let's do it again," he says.

"Vim," he says, calling after me as I walk away.

• • •

GIN AND TONIC, heart of lime, a creaking on the stairs.

Different thing down here. The underworld. Two bare bulbs hang at opposite ends of the room and shadows move as the light moves, the last scene in *Psycho,* third-to-last scene, Vera Miles recoiling in horror.

"He's whatever he's talkin out his ass."

"I know but when *Bleach* came out I was all over it I was."

"Smitten I don't really use that word but this."

"Coming into the room the rain."

"His body his."

"Pouring."

"Wind and waves on a bone-white beach."

I am pissing in a corner behind the boiler in the basement and absolutely nothing fucking else. The feeling of pissing is whoa the feeling of coming in anti-gravity. Exit the capsule the lights go off in the tiny houses back on planet Earth.

So this is outer space.

Drink in my right hand, dick in the left, shake the drips. Ed's voice again. *No matter how much you wiggle and dance the last few drops end up in your pants.* Come out from my hiding place and she's there and she says, staring, she says, "You've got pee stains on your shorts."

"That is my own business."

"And there's two bathrooms upstairs."

"So? I'm a man. I can piss anywhere I want."

"You're a what?"

"Whip it out anywhere and go tinkle."

"I can piss anywhere too."

"Yeah but it's, you're crouching. You gotta crouch."

"Why'd you run off?"

"You gotta crouch, gotta wipe. Whole different thing."

"I was looking forward to sharing another dance."

"So dance with your boyfriend."

"What are you, some tough guy all of a sudden?"

"No but I'm."

"Some lone wolf?"

"No but I'm thirsty. Why don't you run up and get daddy another drink."

"Are you insane?"

"Gin and tonic, baby. 7-Up of the gods."

"You're insane."

"Am I? Or am I totally fucking fine and normal?"

"Totally confused is what you are."

"Hey I'm not the one who prays to William Burroughs."

The ceiling is the floor is throbbing. Picture the dancers crashing through. Picture the house imploding, breaking apart. Picture slivers in my eyes and nails in the rest of me. Picture all these dead hands sticking out of the rubble with their message to the living. *Fuk U.*

YOU ARE OUTSIDE AGAIN, HIDDEN. You are a shadow or an unruly hedge. Helene is the sweetness of the air itself. But why is she with you?

"You worship rock stars," she says.

"Rock stars?"

"Kurt Cobain is a rock star. Get used to it."

"Okay but J Mascis?"

"My point is what's the difference?"

"My point at least my guys are still alive."

"So is William Burroughs."

"He is? That fossil?"

"Lives in Kansas."

"That piece of dust?"

"I'm gonna visit him someday."

"But what about okay didn't he murder his wife? What if god murdered you? How would you feel?"

"God will murder me, smart guy. It's called death."

"This is what you fucking think about?"

"Not usually but."

"Shit, listen."

"What?"

"The Violent Femmes, 'Blister in the Sun.'"

"So?"

"So this album. It's one of those things. Listen to this album and unlock the secrets of my whole . . . being, my whole existence."

"Yeah you and every other."

"Wait, listen."

"Blister in the Sun" ends and it's like the DJ hears your thoughts because he lets the record play next song is "Kiss Off."

You are a spark or a gathering storm. Helene is the end of the long march of time. Emboldened by music, you reach out. You touch her arm.

"What are you doing?" she says, not moving away, she says, "what?"

"I wanna kiss you."

"Tough shit."

"Just one little tiny little kiss."

"You can't."

"Just a nothing little . . . one kiss."

"No."

"One kiss and that'll be it forever. Please don't say no."

"Already said it."

Your fingers move slowly over her skin, her scars, to the back of her hand. "One question. Where's Wheeler?"

"Where? He's inside with Jake he's."

"Why aren't you with Wheeler?"

You lean down, closer, closer, close enough now to feel the heat of her breath on your mouth, and to taste it, sweet and vaguely smoky. You are the drift of days and the unknown future. She's an academy of eyes. Your hands move slowly up her arms. You want to rip out her scars and eat them like Twizzlers.

She says, "This is not going to happen."

You whisper, "One kiss."

The moon, the night, the scars, the song.

You say, "I know who did this."

"Did what?"

"Hurt you. I know who cut you. And I know why."

She smiles. "Come here," she says.

"I'm here."

"Come closer."

Closer, closer, so close your voices touch.

She says, "Vim."

"I'm here."

She says, "You don't know *anything*."

Then she's gone.

Poof.

JACK DANIEL'S AND GINGER ALE and another Bell's and another Bell's. I am drinking and spitting and screaming and dancing between two different worlds and oh I guess that's about it really. I'm telling you now for real I'm telling you that's my life this second and there's nothing more than life this second unless fuck it unless you count the shit of the past and the death of the future and the shit you forgot and the pain you remember and the dreams that you stifle the music you make the life you surrender the world you're resigned to the job that'll kill you the girls who don't like you the dad who left you the mom who raised you the schools that fail you the stepdad who saved you the dreams that mock you the death that awaits you the love that escapes you and the love that'll find you in a world that just fucking doubts you and the pain of this second the pain of this second the pain of the next one too.

JAKE IS HERE. He says: "You want me to hold the chicken?"

I say: "I want you to hold it between your knees."

Wheeler is here, hand on my shoulder, pulling me toward him, speaking into my ear, saying, "I don't, I mean I don't know what it is about her but it's like I've never, I don't think I've ever felt this way about a girl before."

"Great," I say, "terrific fine bravo."

Jake says, "What's that?"

"He says he's never felt this way."

"About what?"

Wheeler says, "Do you know what I mean though?"

"A girl? Shit."

I say, "I've felt the same since fifth grade."

Now the music stops and all movement stops and the crowd quiets. The chemistry of the air changes before the air rushes out of the house. Red lights flash across the walls. I hear a man's voice, amused but also heavy with authority.

"All right, folks."

That's all it takes. People are leaving, pushing past me, walking out the back door, through the yard, through the neighbor's yard, over to Davis Street.

"Whose house is this?"

Jake and Wheeler and Helene are ghosts. Gone. I'm a stranger again.

I walk into the other room. One, two, three, four cops. Two in the living room, two on the porch.

"Who lives here?"

I want to throw myself away.

Wake up dead.

Start over tomorrow.

"Officers," I say.

The one looks but can't really see me. There's a crowd and I'm at the back of the crowd. Gruber Dills stands by the cop. He says, "Dude, don't you need like a, like a what the fuck, like a warrant or something?"

"Son, is this your house?"

"I am a renter," Gruber says.

"Gentlemen," I say, moving through the crowd now. I've got a single dollar bill pinched between my index and middle fingers. Got my hand in the air, the air is heavy, the room is spinning and I am helpless, can't not do this. I've got the dollar bill. I say, "Gentlemen, I think this has all been a big misunderstanding."

Someone touches my arm, says quietly, urgently, "No." Pulls my arm down.

"But we can fix this," I say, smiling.

The girl, whoever, says, "Shut up and follow me."

She leads me through the kitchen, out the back door, through the yard, through the neighbor's yard. And then we're on Davis and the Big Fuck You is history.

THIS WAY, she says.

Or maybe I think.

But who are you?

We hike the cracked concrete steps to East Campus. I know I know her but from where? She's wearing a tie-dye. Shit. Birkenstocks. The ankles aren't fat exactly but. Hair in a long ponytail. Pretty hands from this angle.

"Fuck it," I say.

"Tired?"

"No."

"Almost there," she says, a little winded.

Then silence and climbing. Near the top the staircase narrows and slips into shadows and branches and vines brush against us and we come out bathed in the light of arc sodium lamps. Here is East Hall. Around back are the steps and she sits in the center between two giant pillars. I stand at the edge of the lane at the drop-off and look out over the practice field the stillness so complete the goal posts in the end zones seem ready to come alive and kill and I look up and there's all of Kalamazoo blinking in the distance as if saying *I'm a city too!* almost a skyline the Kalamazoo Building the Comerica Building the Radisson plus straight ahead the lone highrise apartment tower where the nuts went to live when they closed the state hospital.

Malcom X, he had a mom. Malcom X's mom.

Lost her lost her mind.

Mrs. X oh well.

"I love it up here," she says. "Kalamazoo always looks so much . . . bigger."

I'm digging the view and yet not. Helene is somewhere out there in it. Queen Helene, I'll sing when I see her. Sing her to sleep whisper into the flesh of her cheek when she wakes up crying her tears taste like words.

"Were you trying to get arrested?"

"Was I what?"

"Bribing a cop?"

"Not much of a bribe." I take out a dollar and tear it into tiny little bits that blow away in the wind. "See?"

"Wow. Is this like your magic trick? Are you gonna put it together again and like pull it out from behind my ear?"

"No. It's gone forever and who cares."

"Not you, apparently."

"Nope. Don't give two shits. Here, come here."

"What?"

"Gimme your money."

She laughs.

"Come on, cough it up."

"I don't think so."

"Come on, gimme at least a dollar. Be with me on this. Get on the team and get something done." Up the steps now, smiling, hand extended.

"No, for christsake, what."

"One buck."

"All right," she says, "stop, if it'll shut you up, fine." She leans back, digs in her pocket, hands me a wrinkled bill. I flatten it on the pillar, smooth it over, try to make it new again. It's raining money over Kalamazoo.

"WHAT'S YOUR DEAL with Desert Storm?"

Sitting next to each other, knees touching.

"My deal?"

"Yeah, we were talking at the party and you just, you got so riled up about it."

A pause as the scene clicks into focus. Of course. She and her friend.

"Figured there was some, I don't know, something," she says.

Then we kiss. Tongues touch. Open mouth on open mouth. Sounds like a baby chewing bananas but who started it?

"I'm Trudy." Her wet bottom lip reflects a starscape.

"I'm Vim."

"What kinda name's that?"

"Not any kind of a name. It's a nickname."

"How'd you get it?"

Shaking my head.

"Tell me."

"When I was a kid I couldn't, when I was a baby, I couldn't say Vince."

"You sound like what the fuck's that book? My real name being Philip or whatever it is. I took Brit lit last semester."

"So what's Trudy?"

"Short for Gertrude. My grandmother's name."

More kissing, plus my hand under the shirt up the tight little rolls no bra a line of wetness under the tit. A bit of massage or squeezing or what am I doing as she pulls away she looks at me and says, "Vim, do you wanna walk me home?"

NOBODY NOWHERE BUT THE CLERK in Dairy Mart trapped at the counter he floats in brightness the light at Lovell and Oakland has switched to blinking red.

Which way is home, my home? First Trudy's, then mine.

Malcom X, he had a mom she lost her lost her mind.

Up Academy Street we cut through the quad through Kalamazoo College the dark rolling lawn and the chapel's bright white steeple scrapes the sky's edge.

"Do you go to Western?" she says.

"Kind of. I mean, yes. In the fall."

"Really? I graduate this fall. I can't wait."

We keep walking.

"So did you transfer or something?"

"Well."

Then West Main and the cars rushing by and it's just up here on the left, she says. I'm turning away and she touches my arm. Hey wait. Kissing my neck. Wanna come in for a minute? Uh. Touches my face. What's a matter? No nothing it's just. I don't bite, she says. Kisses me we're kissing the cars rush by headlights are the future and taillights the past. She whispers into my neck, I don't bite.

And my erection knows before I do.

Alas, it says, we have traveled this far together, Captain, and she is the one.

IN HER HOUSE, IN HER BEDROOM, squashed in a blue beanbag chair on the floor. She's on top of you. Takes her hair out of the ponytail. Leans down. Smells like shampoo and smoke. The room is patchouli and strawberry incense. Your lungs in your throat, her tongue on your teeth.

"How old are you?" she says.

A pause. Your hand on her bare shoulder. Headlights through the open windows passing over her face and tits like light from falling stars. Pushing into her. Dry humping through shorts through however many drinks still it's a miracle you haven't come yet. "Seventeen."

"Oh my."

"How old are you?"

"Twenty-two."

"I'll be eighteen in August."

"Good to know. I'll be twenty-three in December."

"It started on my birthday."

"What did?"

"Operation Desert Shield. Started August second."

"So is that the deal?" she whispers.

"That is the deal."

Her mouth on your earlobe.

     •   •   •

"WAIT," you say, shaking.

"What?"

"Hold on."

You lift your ass, she pulls off your shorts. "Tighty whities?" she says.

"Yes. For support."

Your face burns in the darkness you wish you wore boxers. You're naked now except for the socks, first time a girl or anyone has seen you naked. Thoughts fly out and swirl and collide to the rhythm of traffic and hang in the air reflecting your heart's deep terror. Her mouth and hair and hand down there, hair draped over your stomach. You cover your eyes with your hands, afraid to look.

"Wait."

"It's okay."

"No come here." And she does and you say, "Malcom X's mom."

"What?"

"Did you know that Malcom X's mom went crazy and they put her in the State Mental Hospital on Oakland Drive and he'd visit her there when he was a kid and."

Her mouth against yours curving into a smile. She says again softly, "It's okay." Then she takes off her shorts.

Here before you above you blue outline of flesh in shifting shadow framed against the rest of your life falling away is a naked woman holy unbelievable shit a naked woman.

     •   •   •

SHE GRIPS IT AND MANEUVERS. Pause. Wait.

Fucking I am fucking I am fucking I am fucking I am not yet fucking I am trembling every muscle stutters as if shocked.

She's crouched above me then easing down and there's moisture but I'm not sure what kind, maybe from her mouth, and pubic hair scratching and "Oh," she sighs but am I penetrating am I fucking am I getting AIDS?

Then a vague flicker bursts into atom-bomb flash bleaching earth and sky as every second of human existence charges out of me into the room and come hits my shoulder chest and cheek and splatters onto the wall behind us like drops of mercury.

Trudy lies down on me our stomachs heave against one another tits pressed warm and slick against my chest. I slip through a trapdoor to childhood watching TV I see an old denture commercial finger bonded by a strip of superadhesive whatever to dentures like a row of blank tombstones.

I have no idea what just happened.

There's a black hole instead of the last two minutes.

Welcome to sex, I'm thinking, this dim wet cave.

Trudy shifts and curls into my arm.

SNAP AWAKE FROM A FRACTURED SLEEP sometime later, Trudy next to me, still nude, snoring faintly, fingers clasped loosely on her belly, the room bathed in the faint gray light of another dawn. I get out of bed and grab my shorts, the only thing I didn't put back on in the move from the floor, and walk quietly to the living room. For a long time I stand at the window and watch the cars. I watch the dead strip mall across the street.

Grab On to Me Tightly as if I Knew the Way

Tiffany's Party Store, Carousel Ice Cream, Papa John's Pizza.

Then I'm on the couch, looking up, and the sun is fully out now, almost colorlessly bright, and the brightness pulses in hard-edged waves and little pieces of dreams come together on the ceiling and fall endlessly apart and I'm dimly aware, somewhere, of my own simple-machine heart beating a rhythm into this chaos.

The world recedes to a pinprick of light and then nothing.

18

How are you not on the floor right now dying after all the funny shit we said about our friends, our friends who we hate, our friends who hate us, who lead us into the waking world hanging on a spit over flame the way your bones will bend and eventually break and your heart'll stop all plugged with grease and the bedsprings were squeaking on a night in winter in '73 and they made you this way and they made you this way and they made you this way too, with bellies slapping and sweat streaming on pale skin and the unremarkable cock so ready to fire and oh baby bang, there, there it was, the moment of your conception.

19

Working the pussy like a five-year-old filling out a job application.

20

"We had a fifth of I think it was Wild Turkey or one of those cheap-shit whiskeys so we were fucked out in about less than five minutes flying down 94 in Al's sister had this monster rusted-out piece of shit station wagon she let him borrow sometimes, fucking thing was about as long as a battleship and Al gunned it all the way to Cobo Hall and we smoked some grass and slammed that fifth so yeah in about five minutes we were fucked for all time. But that was the point, man, that was part of the whole deal, I mean we were on our way to see the Doors and Jim Morrison was our god and nothing we could have shoved into our bodies, no earthly substance, could have possibly been enough. Death itself would not have been enough. I shit you not. For us to die on the way to a Doors concert, crashed in some runoff ditch on 94, with the car flipped and burning and our lips blowing death bubbles in an inch of standing water, well that would have been the ultimate. Yeah break on through. But we made it there, man, obviously or you wouldn't be hearing this, and I remember surprisingly a lot of it, almost the whole night. Al and I walked in after the opening band, who that's the one thing I forget was who the opening band was and this was after we smoked some more grass in the parking lot with some people we met but I remember just the electricity and the energy of waiting and knowing that Jim Morrison was there at that second in the very same building as me. It was a sold-out show and the crowd while the lights were up sounded pretty much like a few thousand pissant shoot-the-shit conversations, like just a lot of chatter. When the lights went down, though, it was like a fucking, like a supersonic jet taking off in my ear and just this *explosion,* this *power* I could feel in the center of my being. You've had that dream, I'm sure. Every asshole who ever strummed a G chord has had that dream, whether they admit it or not. And whatever, Vim, you can tell me how punk or alternative music or whatever you call it isn't about being famous or whatever till you're fucking blue in the face. But I *know,* man. I'm the one who *taught* you and it was an unspoken part of my teachings. Learn guitar, shoot some beaver. So the lights go out and the crowd's shit flips and Ray Manzarek comes out and sits down and Robby Krieger and John Densmore, and you think the noise, that that's as loud as it could possibly get, until here comes Jim, and we're talking this isn't "Light My Fire" Jim or the weird Oedipal rant thing Jim. This is like beer-gut wanna-be blues guy Jim. But it's him in the flesh for real, is the point, and the crowd kicks it up to that next level, whatever level comes after totally fucking apeshit crazy. I don't even know where Al is anymore, I'm totally alone in the middle of this and I'm ready to shit or piss myself or have a heart attack, first of all because I'm so fucked out and second because here's my hero, in the flesh, you know, breathing the same air as me. So he stands there a while, staring into all this madness, looking out at the whole crazy scene which he's seen before about a thousand times and to him probably isn't even all that insane. Then he grabs the mic and goes, with that Voice, you know, we all know the Voice, he goes *Did everybody have a good shit today?* And the band breaks into "Roadhouse Blues" and the drums kick in and Jim unleashes this scream, this wild, unhinged scream of new life kind of thing, and he falls to the floor, like violently throws himself against the floor, and I felt, Vim, it'll sound like bullshit to you but I felt saved. I felt destroyed and put back together again all in the same moment. I just felt, like I said I felt saved. From everything. From myself and my parents and friends and all everybody's *expectations* and my own fucking half-baked expectations and most of all saved from the feeling I had of being dropped down onto the planet without even a vague clue as to how to go about getting through the days, never mind the years, never mind a lifetime, but the *days*. Saved, man. Music saved me. I mean, your mom and I were raised Catholic. Catholic school, confirmation, Christ wafers, the whole shit. Uh-uh, no dice. It was that scream that saved me. But it wasn't quite salvation, though, if that makes any sense, because things for me got real fucked up for a long time after that. Still, no matter how bad it got, and to be honest with you I'm not exactly sure how bad it got since there's about a ten-year period there that's still pretty hazy, but no matter what kind of shit I got myself into, it never once occurred to me to drop to the floor and give a shout-out to the man upstairs. Never once. Because fuck it, man, because why say a prayer when you're already saved?"

21

A few days before he moved up north Uncle Bro came over and gave me a beat-up no-name acoustic guitar, a mildewed Mel Bay chord book, a couple of picks and a spare set of strings. He taught me the G, C and D chords, then wrote out the pentatonic blues scale and said to me, "Play all this till your fingers bleed."

"Okay sure," I said, "just like the Bryan Adams song."

"What?"

"Like the part in the Bryan Adams song where he says he got his guitar and played it till his fingers bled."

Bro paused a moment then as if thinking deeply. He fixed me with a look and said, "Vim, don't take this the wrong way or anything but don't ever fuckin mention the name Bryan Adams to me again."

I was twelve, thirteen, something like that.

22

For a long time I would go to bed late. I had *Are You Experienced* in tablature and spent whole nights learning to play those songs sitting on the couch under a single light in the living room. Sometimes I'd pause, the fingers of my left hand humming, buzzing all the way up into my arm, and there'd be no music and the only sound then was the whistle of trains passing over the tracks in Quincy and it was such a lonely aching lovely sound that I took it to bed and it became a part of me.

23

A broad patch of grass on the far end of the lawn has yellowed. The dirt beneath it is dusty and dry. I walk out into the dark woods behind our house and lose myself in the tangles and shifting shadows. I have known these trees my whole life. I have bled, died and been reborn here in kid games with plastic guns, invisible bullets, the soft earth always there to break my fall. The leaves, my friends, they wink at me as the sunlight flickers between branches. The breeze in the treetops sounds like the ocean.

And when I get back Ed's home from work standing with his back to me, leaning over the sink, staring into the drain. He inhales deeply and sighs out his breath.

"How you doin?" I say.

"Okay," his voice low, "just tired, is all."

"How was, how was work?"

"Ah same shit."

"Same shit, different day," I say, hoping to let in some light.

"Nope." He empties his blue Igloo lunch cooler, starts rinsing out the thermos and Tupperware. "Same shit, same day."

24

My chest is constantly warm and tight. A stuck alarm clock blares inside me, buried somewhere deep. Every heartbeat, every endless second, I hang from the walls, drop to the floor, fall out of my dreams into awful daylight. I wander back behind the Hobart and wait for the shitstorm and Wendell's there singing *take me down to the Paradise City where the grass is green and the girls are pretty oh won't you please take me home* . . .

25

He showed up on Thursday, the night before graduation, drove a rental from his sister's in some Chicago suburb. He's gained maybe forty pounds since the last time I saw him, which I guess was his wedding over two years ago. He looks like Benny, the retarded mail boy from *L.A. Law*, same hairline, mouth, body shape. His belly sticks out like a beach ball and when we hug with hard backslaps our bodies sound hollow.

I can smell his neck. Drakkar Noir.

So my father wears the same cologne as every asshole I went to school with.

He and my mom hug politely, barely touching, two shirts brushing together on a laundry line. He and Ed shake hands.

"Hey Ed, good to see you."

"Hey Joe, good to see you too."

And then we're all just fucking standing in the kitchen.

He and Ed have met before, of course, not sure when, maybe something like ten years ago, back in the days when I still said I love you too at the end of his occasional phone calls. There was always something fake in his voice, not malicious or deceitful, but like *Hey ha everything's fun we're pals,* till after a while all I could hear were the silences between words, the miles between us, the distance.

My mom says, "Well you're looking good, Joe."

But what the fuck, I'm thinking, has she ever seen *L.A. Law*?

"How's Meredith?"

For a second I can't remember but Meredith is his wife, technically my stepmom. I was at their wedding. It rained that day the rain slashed sideways in cold metallic sheets that blew through the outdoor reception like an omen.

They live in Baltimore with two cats.

"Meredith's good, she's . . . she sends her best." And he looks at me and says, "God, a high school graduate. Seems like just last, I mean like just yesterday. And now you know . . . wow I can't believe it." He looks at my mom and grins and says: "Can you believe it, Anne?"

A silence, broken first by the electric hum of the refrigerator and then my mother's voice saying: "Actually, yeah, Joe, I can."

Her face is frozen in a smile.

Ed steps toward the refrigerator, he leans in and squints. "Seems like there's a rattle comin from somewhere. Vim, you hear a rattle? No? I'll take a look later maybe, get in there and dink around."

What are you, Ed, some genius of metaphor? The rattle comes from us, the three of us like poles on a highway connected head-to-head by high-tension power lines and the past is a current charging between particles raising the hairs on my neck.

WE PULL INTO THE BAYVIEW—*TRY OUR PERCH BEST IN TOWN NECESSITY IS THE MOTHER OF INVENTION*—just my dad and me in his rented car with the dangling pine air freshener. He looks at my knees touching the dash and chuckles and says: "No status in a Stratus."

The sad empty dance floor streaked with fading sunlight. The empty stage. The rowboat salad bar with plastic ladles sticking up. The corpselike waitress with a shriveled orange face approaching, trailing the dust of the ages.

"What can I get ya?"

"Food, lots of food," my dad says, "or should I be more specific?"

"Oh ya think," she says, laughing loudly, a deep cackling smoker's laugh that stirs some wetness. "Maybe just this much," she says, raising a hand with finger and thumb a little apart. He orders ribs, I get the shrimp scampi and the old girl disappears.

I unfold my napkin, refold it, tear it in two, gaze out the window, out at the ship, look over at the bar, the bartender's hair, the beer guy hauling in cases of Bud Light on a dolly. My dad asks about the band and what else have I been up to and what's the girl situation and how goes the job. He tells me about the great deal he got on a hotel, which really, it's not like a hotel at all, it's more like separate apartments, not far from the Western Michigan campus, which I drove through on the way to the house today and it looks like a pretty campus and you're, you said you're gonna live in a dorm, right? Uh-huh uh-huh. And what do you think you're gonna study? No I know, there's still plenty of time for that, plenty of . . . time to figure it all out, you know I didn't declare a major till I guess it was my junior year. Now didn't you, you said you looked at Michigan State too, right? Well I imagine it's changed quite a bit since I was, since your mother and I were there. Or maybe not or. Some things, you know it's the old cliché, some things never. Or else the more they change the more they. You've changed though, no question. You look good, Vim, you're looking. Well I just mean you're looking grown-up. Your face and your, everything about you really, it's like you're a, god you're a grown man now. And it's terrifying. Ha ha. No I know maybe that's the wrong word but it's like I was telling your mother it's, one minute you're uh . . . you're . . .

26

I'd been asleep I don't know how long, maybe ten minutes, maybe an hour, all of it restless, dreamless, and then I heard a throat clearing, a toilet, a faucet, footsteps creaking on a hardwood floor. And then someone was standing over me.

Hey.

My eyelids click when they open and I feel every vein,

jagged red and choking. It's Trudy upside down, uncombed hair hanging in her face, wearing a U2 T-shirt with cutoff sleeves. Oh my god. Who is this person and what have we done together?

"Hey," she says again.

"Hi." My voice barely a whisper, tongue swollen and dry. Every taste bud feels as big as a plate. I clear my throat and say: "I don't think I can move."

She says: "Here lemme help you."

And then whoa, I'm upright again and the old blood is working.

I can't believe I'm still alive.

Trudy sits and together we look out the window.

"Are you hungry?" she says.

"Water," I say.

"Hydration. Good idea. Wait here."

She comes back with two plastic McDonald's Supersize cups filled with still-fizzing tap water. I drink it all down in a couple gulps and instantly have to piss.

"Is there a . . . bathroom?"

She points the way, swishing water in her mouth, and slowly I stand. The bathroom feels like about ten miles away. There is a mirror. I look like an abortion. My piss is a pale reeking rope. *A beanbag chair, Trudy above me, headlights, titties, terror.* But did I do fucking? I fight the urges to puke and cry and climb out the window and wander shoeless back to wherever I came from.

On the coffee table is more water, an assortment of tablets.

Trudy says: "Take these. We got Tylenol here, a B-12, some vitamin C . . ."

More footsteps. I turn around. A strange girl smiling slyly. But wait, she's no stranger. Her face comes back. Of course. The other Desert Storm girl.

"Hey you're that guy," she says. "I mean kid. Jeez."

I say: "Yeah that's me. The Kid."

"Had some kinda bug up your ass about Desert Shield or whatever?"

I say: "Right."

The girl has a three-foot water bong and starts doing hits. She says: "Wake and bake is fun."

In observance of good pot etiquette, she offers us the bong. Trudy smiles and declines and I am *this* close to spraying the entire world with vomit. Those pills I took are sitting in my empty stomach like three lead turds.

"So Vim," Trudy says, "did you say you were hungry?"

"Vim?" from the other girl.

"Vim," I say.

"Vim," Trudy says.

"Now everybody," I say.

I say: "Hungry? Uh yeah. Sure. I guess."

"Well then it looks like we're going out because all I have here is Yoo-hoo and Cocoa Puffs."

And then we're speeding along in her little red car with PC commands all over it. *Keep Your Laws Off My Body. Love Your Mother. Visualize World Peace. Free Leonard Peltier.* We take a left on Drake, go down to Stadium and turn into the Big Boy. Look at that fat plastic fucker, still holding up his prized burger with his idiot smile.

The all-you-can-eat breakfast buffet is kind of a miracle and kind of a nightmare. The place is packed with all the chain-smoking foreign students who stay in town after school lets out. Trudy has a large Coke *and* an orange juice *and* a water *and* a coffee. She eats scrambled eggs like cake crumbs, trapping little dry bits in her fork tines.

She says: "So what happened to you last night?"

I say: "In what sense do you mean that?"

"Well, you sleep with me and then when I wake up you're gone?"

She sips from one of her four beverages.

"Yeah," I say, "about that . . ."

"Yeah?"

My mouth hangs open but no words come. I am so fucking tired, so young and stupid and useless and sick. I feel like sex, or even just the idea of sex, crawled into me and died like a squirrel in an attic, and it's now giving off foul death odors.

Trudy says: "Why'd you disappear?"

I smile and say: "Isn't that what men do?"

She looks at me with pity or anger. "Yeah," she says, "some of them."

Then we eat in silence, making alternate trips to the buffet. No one comes by to clear our table and by the third or fourth trip we're surrounded by plates with waffles and pancakes and all different meats, everything encrusted in syrup.

"By the way," she says, "breakfast is on me."

Which is good to hear because all my money is torn in shreds in the high grass on the side of the East Campus hill.

27

The house is so bright, the air is so still, so fragrant, the kitchen smells faintly of coffee, of cooking. A pan on the range filled with water to soak. Little bits of egg floating in the water. My hands are as light as dead leaves.

I walk into the living room and my mother is there on the couch in her nightshirt and sweatpants. *Car Talk* on the radio, scattered sections of the Sunday *Gazette*.

The day is so bright, so beautifully shot through with mid-morning light I can't remember a day as blinding as this one. Out back through the window the woods and the swamp and the blue and white sky touching down in the distance.

My mother is on the couch looking over as I stand in the doorway confused by the light and the heat. I only want to take a shower and sleep. She puts down the paper and picks up her coffee cup. She laughs a little. I smile a tired smile. A bee flies into the screen and bounces away. The wind blows and rustles the pages of the Sunday paper.

I want to take a ten-year shower. There is the night to wash off me, all the doubt and the dark things lingering. I feel naked in the brightness now, exposed, like my skin is peeling off and I'm showing her everything, for the first time showing my mother my heart, my fear, the sunken bruises that never heal.

She leans forward on the couch, still smiling. Neither of us has spoken. We are engulfed in this wondrous silence, a moment both expanding and already gone.

Then the spell is broken. I sit in the chair and take a breath. My mother says: "So what happened to you last night?"

28

Now sporting boxers in a variety of styles—plaid, stripes, pea-green polka dots, name it—ready to face the world like a man.

29

Ellroy Marx, the Kalamazoo Scene God, nearly thirty, dangerously thin, equally revered and despised, wears a T-shirt with the famous Iwo Jima picture on it, but instead of Old Glory, the marines raise the Golden Arches over the words *America: Billions and Billions Served*. He also has a Public Enemy hat, I guess to prove he's down with the Struggle.

Hole in Your Head is his joint, half record store, half all-ages club, a kind of splintery punk rock Honeycomb Hideout run by whoever he can swindle into working for free. Over the years he's started and lost about five different versions of it. They call him Scene God because he books the shows and hosts the touring bands and cruises the streets in his silver Taurus staple-gunning homemade fliers all over the place. The one for today's show has a picture of an Ewok with a gun to its face.

At some point *Star Wars* became the new punk religion. Look around. Plenty of "Yoda Was Vegan" patches and Rebel Alliance tattoos. Many breathless debates about which is the better film, the first one or *Empire*. I don't fucking get it.

"Dude do you have Boba Fett still in the box?"

"No I stuck my Boba Fett in the dirt and broke his arms off back in like 1980."

"In other words . . . "

"Yes. It was a toy. I played with it."

A gaggle of emo kids with backpacks, bleached hair, giant jeans. A guy with Rites of Spring drawn in marker on his triple-XL T-shirt. Another guy has Soul Side. Jawbreaker, the Morton salt girl. *When it pains, it roars*. Fat black Xs painted on hands.

"Did you get the new Death Star seven-inch?"

"No."

"What you're kidding me shit what about the Liars in Love LP?"

"Uh-uh."

"Tell me you at least got the Violent Apathy reissue?"

"Well I could tell you that but it wouldn't be true."

"The Dick Divers single?"

"Doesn't ring a bell."

"You're kidding me right that's a joke right?"

"It's not I guess I wish it was."

"What the fuck is the matter with you?"

"Oh I don't know. A few different things."

Ellroy's eating a Domino's pizza with all the cheese scraped off and pretzels crushed on top. A sign above his head says *The*

Ellroy Marx Sweet Quote of the Century "Nirvana Stayed At My House, Motherfucker."

"Is it true, Ellroy?"

"What?"

"That Nirvana stayed at your house."

"Fuck yes it's true, motherfucker. Nirvana, Club Soda, 1989. Where were you?"

"Well let's see. Pretty tough to account for a whole year."

"It was October. It was raining. I had just turned twenty-four. I was listening to Django Reinhardt and rereading favorite passages from Plato's *Republic*. But yeah whatever, I booked Nirvana for a Monday New Music Night. One of the lesser SubPop bands, was my opinion then. The 'Love Buzz' single didn't really kill me. Neither did their song on the SubPop 200 comp. After the show they came to my house and we all watched *Zapped!* Ben Shepherd from Soundgarden was their roadie. The Lyle Lovett–looking motherfucker. Every asshole in Kalamazoo now claims to have been at that show but let's be clear. I was there. I have pictures. It was me, Finch the bartender and a drunk guy at the front of the stage playing a Jew's harp. Cobain stole twenty-six dollars and eighty-seven cents off my dresser. No shit. That fucker owes me money and if I ever see him again I'm gonna ask for it back. Do you have the new Rilke's Jissom record yet? No? Fuck. It's their best shit since *Alone in the Clock Tower With My Rifle Drawn*."

Freshman punks sucking clove cigarettes, staring sullenly at the floor as if the answers to life's mysteries were written in the grime there.

Jake fiddling with his tuner on the plywood stage.

A girl with fifteen facial piercings passing out a photocopied pamphlet entitled *Same Sex Spousal Abuse: What You Can Do To Break the Cycle.*

"Aren't there more pressing social problems?"

"Maybe in the straight world, what. You wanna debate?"

"Absolutely, honey baby, just give me one quick second."

Green Day on the PA and someone's talking shit about how they saw them at Sgt Pepperoni's with Damone and Death to Endor.

"Yeah that's cool but I saw them play at the Pole Barn in Otsego with Spitboy and Spork in front of maybe like ten or twelve people."

"No you didn't dude I was at that show they didn't show up."

"Fuck you yes they did."

"The show where Id Scalini took a crack on the head with a forty bottle and sat in the grass pulling glass bits from his skin with only the light from his Zippo?"

"Right."

"The one where Rock Bottom Renee gave head to whoever for a dollar till she saved up enough for a chocolate éclair and a nickel bag?"

"That's the one."

"I got news for you dude Green Day was nowhere near the Pole Barn that night."

"Fuck you yes they were."

"I heard they left Lookout! and signed to a major."

"Nope no way I know Billie Joe I've talked to him personally and all I can say to you about that is no over and over again no."

Wheeler's all over the place, shifting from one foot to the other. He cracks his knuckles, chews his nails, twists his hair.

"What's the matter with you?"

"I'm nervous, man. For real."

"Really? Where's Helene?"

"She's," scanning the crowd, "there she is."

Talking to a girl on the other side of the room, both of them laughing, smoking. I hate smoking. Bad memories of my mom in her single days. Yet the way Helene looks now, head tilted, lips parted . . . well I could learn to like anything, couldn't I?

Wheeler wipes his hands on his shirt. "Seriously, what if I can't hold the sticks? What if I fuck up and the show's a disaster and it's all on me?"

"That won't happen."

"What if it does?"

"Come on, now you're making *me* nervous."

"You weren't already?"

"Yeah. Yeah I really was."

More kids file in, they look younger and younger. More homemade T-shirts. Bad Brains, Black Flag, Born Against, Misfits, Social Distortion, Circus Lupus, NOFX, Nation of Ulysses, Fugazi and Fugazi, always Fugazi. All the budding riot grrls, braless with nipple boners, dyed hair, jagged hacked bangs and bright red lipstick.

"Who's the better poet, Jim Morrison or Henry Rollins?"

"Hey go easy."

"No, go vegan."

"Yeah Yoda was vegan."

Like it says on the T-shirt like it says on your face like it says on your heart on your sleeve on your bedroom wall on the cover of your zine on your bumper sticker.

Jake leans against his amp. He raises a fist and pumps it slowly with an athlete's casual confidence. The room is heavy with smoke, hot with people. The crowd parts for Ellroy like he's got a golden staff, a footlong beard and ten stone tablets.

"Do the math, dude, without Jim Morrison there's no Iggy Pop."

"So?"

"Without Iggy Pop there's no punk rock."

"Oh."

"It's time," Ellroy says. He points at his wrist, at the bare skin there.

Jake, already strapped on, plays the bass line to "Ceremony" as a warm-up. He always does, even at practice. New Order, an old family favorite. A few heads turn. A few smiles of acknowledgment, including mine. Wheeler's at the drums, doing all his ritualistic preshow adjustments, pulling his snare closer, pushing it back, tightening cymbals etc. He draws a deep breath and blows on his knuckles, does a few light, jazzy fills.

I am tuning now.

Elephants Always Do Grow Big Ears.

Jake hands me a set list.

"Who wrote this?" I say.

"You did."

I let it drop to the floor.

Some smart-ass put Metallica on the PA. Or maybe, I don't know, it's someone who really just likes Metallica. *Master master where's the dreams that I been after?*

A projector clicks in my head. I watch the flickering countdown. A black thread stutters endlessly over the frame, the bleached image, a blank desert vista. Suddenly the image skips and a bright white hole opens at its center and the edges expand and turn black and the film breaks but the reels keep turning.

The mic whines a little, it feeds back.

Metallica drops off.

My voice fills the room. "Good afternoon. We're the Judy Lumpers."

"Less talk more rock!" someone shouts in the back.

I say: "Did everybody have a good shit today?"

And then four drumstick clicks and here we go.

The first song is "Built Myself But I Exploded." The bass and drums throb into my shins. The power light on the Twin Reverb glows like god's electric blood. The way my hand doesn't know anything with all these faces staring back at me and then it all of a sudden does. My ears ring and my bones shatter and sweat drips into my eyes.

> *Built myself but I exploded*
> *The sun burned out and god eroded*
> *And the crane came and dropped you*
> *Screaming, baby, through this shit world*
> *And right down onto me*
> *Right into my lap.*

I have no idea who the fuck I am but I feel that thing that rages through the past and bangs around your ribs and closes on your heart like a vise.

30

A long nothing stretch out on Sprinkle Road, out past the giant plumbing supplies warehouse with the toilet out front where if the lid's up they're open, if the lid's closed they're closed, out past the quarry and the man-made lake, past the party stores and the Denny's and the brand-new Perkins, past the cluster of motels with giant signage scraping the sky.

Red Roof Inn, Fairfield Inn, Comfort Inn, Quality Inn.

Jake is driving and the van flies along. I'm hanging half out the window with my eyes squeezed shut. The wind fills my body with its great dull roar.

Back inside everything tingles.

"Our music . . . ," I say.

"Yeah?"

"It's such boring copycat shit."

"And your point being?"

"Verse chorus verse chorus bridge chorus end."

"Okay so we stretch it out a little. Like lately I've been listening to this German band, Spills and Bricklayers, real esoteric sixties pre-punk shit with like four trombones, a zither and a chick who plays spoons."

"That's not us, I don't think. Or at least it's not me."

"Oh yeah. What's you?"

"Verse chorus verse chorus bridge chorus end."

"All right so there you have it. Why reinvent the wheel?"

"Fuck reinventing anything, we can't even put in an original spoke."

"Well now hold on there, pal. I think we got a spoke or two in us."

"There's gotta be a more interesting way."

"Trust me, there's not."

"I mean I know we're not the Beatles or anything."

"No fucking shit. Where have you been? We're not even the Dave Clark Five. We're not even the motherfucking Monkees."

"Who are we then? Bobby Sherman?"

"Hey Vim."

"Strawberry Alarm Clock?"

"My man."

"Kajagoogoo?"

"Vim, listen to me."

"What?"

"In the whole history of music?"

"Yeah?"

"In the whole entire history of music, the whole shit, there's only twelve notes. Bam. That's it. Beethoven to the Ramones to us. Twelve notes."

"And your point being?"

"There are only so many ways to tell the same story."

31

There is only one Mollineaux in the Kalamazoo phone book. My hand shakes as I hold the phone. I dial and hang up, dial and hang up. Finally I take a deep breath and I'm ready. Four rings later she answers. "Helene? It's, hi it's Vim. Sweeney."

"Vim Sweeney. What a pleasant surprise."

"Really?"

"No."

"How are you?"

"Fine."

"Good."

"And you?"

"Well," I say.

"Well what?"

"I'm doing well."

"Good."

"So uh, so yeah. Guess I'll see you later."

"Hm. You sure?"

"No," I say, "I am not at all sure. Maybe we should talk now, just for a minute."

"Okay. What about?"

"Anything, you know, just . . . conversate. We'll have an exchange."

"Okay. This is all seeming like . . . very formal."

"Why risk an awkward pause?"

"What do you wanna say to me, Vim?"

"Nothing. I just wanna know you."

I'm in a dark room in the basement. There are plaques with deer antlers jutting from soft red mounds. There is a big mounted bass my mom only recently let Ed move in from the garage. Ed named the fish Buster. There are pictures in frames on a shelf. Ed in his army uniform. Ed's mother. Ed with his brothers and sisters sometime in what's gotta be the '70s, everyone smiling before a painted bookshelf backdrop. Ed as a kid chopping wood in a field with his father. Ed kneeling before a freshly killed deer.

All the lights are off and the window is open.

I am lying on the floor, holding the phone, breathing.

Helene's voice rushes into me.

Her mother isn't home, she works nights at Checker Motors, in the pressroom, punching out rivets. She too has scars on her arms from long ago when they had her on bumpers and the metal cut through the protective arm bands, not all at once, but after a whole night's work, after a few hundred bumpers. OSHA's a joke, says her mother.

"What's OSHA?"

"I think it's like some safety thing."

Her little brother's sleeping. His name is Jordan, not really but that's what he wants to be called, as in Michael, number 23. He's the runt of his friends and a runt in general but still.

"I tell him all the time when the bigger kids tease him that even Michael Jordan didn't make his high school team."

"Is that true?"

"Yeah, I think I heard that somewhere."

"Where would you have heard that?"

"Why? Should I not know that?"

"No but."

She lives in a trailer park called Chateau Acres way out in Portage. They moved there after her parents split. What happened was everything was groovy till it wasn't anymore. Her father was a nice big handsome guy, a partier. He made good money as a roofer. But then one day he tripped and fell off a roof and broke his body and after a long time in the hospital and a long time in bed and a long time on the couch he became another person, depressed and bitter and taking pain pills all the time and then drinking too and things went south pretty fucking fast. They lived in a house in Allegan then. She was ten, her brother was six. Her dad went crazy, flew into rages, flipped over TVs, punched holes in the walls and pissed on the lawn in broad daylight in full view of the neighbors. He never hurt anyone but that seemed to be where things were headed.

So now the trailer.

No one really knows where her father is. He blows in and out of town. Once in a while he turns up at Shorty's or the Green Top or the Studio Lounge or sometimes even their front door on a weekend afternoon, all sober and shaking and a huge smile and beating around the bush and almost but never quite asking forgiveness.

Her mother does her best, does more than her best, but a lot of times her love is misplaced or careless. She still parties all the time with friends from work.

Very early one morning Helene heard a noise. She got up and looked out the window and there was her mother down on her knees in the little patch of grass out front, tearing at the grass and pulling it up.

Mom what the hell are you doing?

Look baby. Diamonds. There's all these diamonds every-where.

Mom what the fuck?

Look baby get out here and help me we're rich.

Her mother had dropped acid, called in sick, closed out the bar and then gone to a friend's house. She had driven home and was about to go in when she noticed dew in the grass sparkling in the porch light.

Come out here baby and help me look.

Helene sat with her mother and together they ran their hands through the wet grass as the sun rose. She says as long as she lives she'll never forget the weird bright sky and the way everything smelled and her mother's tears.

She says, "We shouldn't, I don't think we should be talking like this."

I pretend not to hear. I hold my breath. I say, "Go on."

Her middle name is Marie, after Lisa Marie Presley. Her dad's the Elvis fan, thought it was cool the King named a whole plane after his daughter. For a long time his big dream for a family trip was to drag everyone to Memphis, to Graceland. Come on, bad taste was born there. Helene, you like pink. At Graceland, everything's pink. Hell, where's everyone's sense of adventure?

"Pink?" I say.

"My favorite color," she says.

"Does Wheeler know that?"

"No one knows that."

But they never made it to Graceland. In the end it was al-ways Cedar Point.

"Please," I say. "Don't bring up Cedar Point."

"Why?"

"Long story."

"We have time."

"Not for this, we don't."

"You don't like roller coasters?"

"I wouldn't know. I've never been on one."

"You've never been on a roller coaster?"

"No," I say. "And I don't care. I'll never go. Motherfuck a roller coaster."

"So much anger," she says.

"And motherfuck Cedar Point."

"Such a child of divorce," she says.

"Are you fucking kidding?"

"Is it like some traumatic dad thing where he wouldn't take you to Cedar Point as a kid no matter how much you begged and boo-hooed?"

"As a matter of fact, no."

"I'm just asking."

"As a matter of fact."

"Don't get all pissy, I'm just."

"Are you not angry at your own father?"

A pause. "That's not exactly the word I'd use."

"Okay. What word exactly would you use?"

Longer pause. She sighs. "We shouldn't be talking like this."

"What, a friendly conversation."

"No."

"A casual exchange."

"It's more than that now."

"How do you figure?"

"Don't play dumb."

"First of all, listen."

"I'm with Bixby."

"First of all."

"What?"

"I don't have to play dumb, okay? I *am* dumb."

"Bixby as in your friend, as in the drummer of your band."

"Helene I want you to listen to me very carefully."

"Vim I like you. I do. I like you and I really just wanna."

"Do *not* tell me you just wanna fucking be friends."

Silence on her end of the line and mine too. I have the phone pressed so hard against my ear and I am so alone in this room. After a minute more she says: "I don't wanna just hang up. I wanna say bye first. So please say bye."

But I don't say anything.

"Okay so I'm gonna say it," she says, "and then I'm gonna hang up."

And she's as good as her word.

32

Is it stupid to say you hurt or a problem to wanna cry but you can't or you wanna let go of something bad but you won't? No hey you don't have to answer that. This isn't faith, it ain't a fucking court of law. Stick your pain where the sun don't shine. Oh and one more thing: Is it too early in the game to concede defeat?

Peel slowly and see.

33

Yellow ribbons on the car antennas, big yellow ribbons tied to the trees, fluttering, waving sadly in the breeze. On the Gull Lake High School sign *THOSE IN UNIFORM COME HOM SAFE FRI NITE GULL LAKE VS QUINCY DANCE AFTER GAME.* An awkward moment of silence at the dance for all the brave souls in the desert overseas. Then exorcism—*kick out the jams, motherfucker!*—then lust.

34

And then I masturbated and felt revived.
   I dreamed in some undiscovered language.

35

Schizophrenic horizon. Fat black clouds touching a world so bright it looks on fire. A sudden shift in the atmosphere, the heat sucked out as if through a straw. A hard cool breeze rolls in off the swamp and the blinds blow in and bang against the sills. The air tastes like a screen. Low rumble of distant thunder. The clouds shift and mutate and fly across the sky. A flicker of lightning. The thunder comes closer. The rain begins. It rages down in bullet-sized drops then lets up briefly before leveling off in a dark cascade. The power goes in and out. The fan's blades slow but never quite stop. The clock on the VCR goes black, blinks a dim green twelve. Down the hall a door slams. A magazine blows open on the floor. Another door creaking and then it too slams shut. The thunder so close now it's like semis crashing on the roof. The lightning does not stop. The window panes are splattered with rain. The wind batters the house from every direction as the storm falls through itself.

36

"Vim?" A girl's voice, faint, tired-sounding. I get a pang, a flash of Helene, but know it's not her. "Vim, this is Trudy."

"Oh." Forgot we'd traded numbers. "Hi."

"Do you have a second?"

"Sure."

"Good," she says. "Vim, I have chlamydia."

I'm standing in the kitchen and everything freezes except my mom's hands working a bowl of ground beef. My voice when I finally speak is high and weird, the voice of another different terrified person. "Would you mind . . . repeating that?"

"Please," she says, "don't make me."

"No, do. I really should wanna be clear on this one."

"I have," a strange half sob bursts forth, "I have chlamydia. Okay? There."

"Yeah no, good, thank you, that's . . . that's what I thought you said."

The world slowly unfreezes. My mother's wedding ring is on a plate on the counter on top of some junk mail. Ground beef, when kneaded, makes a sickening loud clicking sound. "So obviously," Trudy says, "there's a chance you have it too."

"Obviously," I say, as if she'd just told me that man had been to the moon.

"I'm sorry this is so embarrassing I just found out today and I called as soon as."

"Okay hold on."

"What?"

"Well this thing you've mentioned. I'm not sure what it is."

Thinking back to sex ed now but all I can remember is a single sentence uttered by the hugely obese Mr Waldbaum, a guy we called Whalebones who otherwise taught history and wore giant turquoise rings on Vienna-sausage fingers and the sentence is ping-ponging around in my head: *Condom, street name rubber.*

"What?" Trudy says.

"I mean I've heard the word before but let's talk."

"It's just, you know, an infection," she says, clearing her throat. "Very minor."

"How minor?"

"Very."

"Please explain."

"Curable with antibiotics. Like if you had strep throat or something."

"Strep throat?" I look down, fully expecting to see my green withered dick fall to the floor and melt into pudding that very second.

"But the thing is, the woman at the health center told me, she said that guys sometimes don't know they have it. So they go years without showing symptoms and if they don't catch it then maybe you know like they might end up . . ."

"Yes?"

"They might go sterile," she says.

"Interesting." I have never exactly longed to have children.

"They gave me a pamphlet," she says.

"Do I own it?"

"Well . . . no, not yet. But I can get you one if you want."

"No, the other thing. The larger thing. Do I own *that*?"

"Well I don't know, I mean like I said, there's a chance."

"What kinda chance, would you say?"

"I really don't know."

"But say if you had to lay odds?"

"Vim."

"Like pretend it's the Rose Bowl."

"Stop it okay I said I don't know!"

"All right, hey no biggie. But just tell me this then."

"What?" she says after a few sniffles.

"How did you come to acquire such a . . . strange little basket of stuff?"

"I don't know, it's . . . fuck. Maybe Percival. My boyfriend."

"Your *what*?"

"Ex-boyfriend. Look it doesn't matter."

"Oh doesn't it?"

"No. The point is . . ."

"Yes? I would like to hear it."

"The point is I thought it was just a yeast infection because I get those sometimes. But you know, so when it didn't go away I went to the doctor. And now this."

"You thought at first what? I'm still very unclear."

She gives me the 411 on yeast infections, then asks if I'm allergic to penicillin. "I'll say I spilled my prescription down the drain or something and they'll write me a new one. That's all they do there is give antibiotics to anyone who sneezes."

"Well that sure sounds like fun," I say.

"What are you doing tomorrow? Like around noon? Hello?"

"Yes. Noon. I'm sorry, what were you saying?"

"Can you meet me at the cemetery on West Main Hill?"

"Ah so it's true," I say. "I really *am* dying."

My mother looks at me. I point at the phone and nod and smile.

Trudy goes on, "There's a really crazy headstone, a giant sphere, way in the back at the loop in the road. That's where I'll be. Vim I'm really sorry I didn't know it never would have happened like that if I'd known."

"Good to know. Comforting. That pleases me."

"I mean obviously if I would have known I'd."

"Okay thanks. Bye."

I walk to the bathroom on crazy insanely shaking legs, get out a magnifying glass and examine my dick, shriveled now to a frightened nub. I stretch it out and move it all around. It looks normal. Ugly in the way that all dicks are ugly, but normal.

There's no pain, no swelling, no redness, no pus. I squeeze the tip and squint at the hole. Nothing. Switch eyes and still nothing. I pull, twist, bend, press, pinch, roll. I don't even know what the fuck I'm looking for.

Finally I get in the shower and scrub myself raw, turning the water hotter every few minutes till the cold is pretty much all the way off and I'm under a scalding spray in a shroud of steam, flossing my nether regions with a series of soapy washcloths.

Never again. No more pussy or almost-pussy.

Later, at the table, my face still red from the heat of the water, dick and ass still tender from all of the scrubbing, wet hair slicked straight back like a fucking extra on *Miami Vice,* Ed says, "Nice of you to get washed up for dinner."

And I'll tell you this right now, no bullshit: Whoever invented meat loaf should be dragged into the street and shot.

37

She's reading a book in the grass by the sphere. She looks up when she hears me approaching and smiles, arm up to shield her eyes from the sun. "Hey," she says. "You made it."

"Are you kidding? I wouldn't have missed this for the world."

I step up onto the edge of the headstone and wrap my arms around the sphere, which is sort of a famous Kalamazoo landmark, about six feet in circumference. I press my cheek against the warm gray marble. In the earth below us lies Marion Raven-wood. "What's that you're reading?" I say.

"Oh. It's this book *A Death in the Family*."

"Never heard of it."

"I hadn't either. My brother gave it to me. He said it would change my life."

"Has it?"

"It could, I guess. Some of it's like reading poetry."

"Poetry. I used to write some of that shit," I say.

"Why'd you stop?"

"I don't know. Maybe I thought poets couldn't compete in the real world."

"Oh? I didn't know the real world was all about competition."

"Maybe it's not. I don't know what it's about. Do you?"

"No. And I think anyone who says they know is lying. Or just like, deluded."

"Well that's a crusher. I was hoping things got clearer with age."

"You mean like you reach a certain point and suddenly a lightbulb goes off and you've magically got your shit together?"

"Something like that."

"I don't think it works that way. I think you're always trying to get it right."

"I am?"

She looks at me. "Okay, I think *one* is always trying to get it right."

We sit for a while. I leaf through her book and come across the lines: "*How far we all come. How far we all come away from ourselves. So far, so much between, you can never go home again.*

You can go home, it's good to go home, but you never really get all the way home again in your life. And what's it all for? All I tried to be, all I ever wanted and went away for, what's it all for?"

"How have you been?" Trudy says. "I mean, otherwise."

"That's a good question," I say, putting down the book.

"I'm not trying to trick you."

"I know."

"This isn't a test."

"I know."

"So?"

"So it's like . . . sometimes I feel like there's only one way to go, just up and up forever. You know? Like I'm a . . . like I'm fucking untouchably great."

"What's it like the other times?"

"Like I have to bash my head against the wall for ten hours just to come up with something to look forward to or be excited about."

"Well that seems . . . normal."

"Does it?"

"To a degree. Maybe everything but the head-bashing part. What about school in the fall? College. Aren't you at least kinda psyched about that?"

"Were you?"

"Yeah. For sure. But only for like a year or two, when everything was like, some new great experience and eating Apple Jacks for dinner every night represented the height of personal freedom. Now I'm way ready to be gone."

"Apple Jacks," I say. "I could go for some of those."

"You never called me," she says.

"I know."

"Why not?"

I can't think of anything to say, so I turn away from her.

"Well let me just tell you this one thing then, okay. It can be your lesson for the day. Girls don't like it when guys don't call. It's not appreciated. Especially after, you know, intimacies have been exchanged."

"Intimacies? Is that what we exchanged?"

"I believe the fluids were mostly yours."

Anger and embarrassment and shame flood through me all at once. "Okay, are we done here? Can I have my pills? Can I go away and die now, please?"

"Hey. Listen," she snaps, and then doesn't say anything for a while. I can tell when she's about to speak because she draws a sharp breath. "One of these days you're gonna have to give up this stupid teenage death-trip shit."

"Oh really? Thanks. Is that my second lesson for the day?"

"No." She lays a hand gently on my shoulder. "Just an observation."

She's prettier than I remember. Her eyes are deep brown, like polished jewels, and there is an openness about her. Ahead of us is a long sloping hill. The cemetery stretches into the distance, rows of headstones and flat crumbling grave markers and mini obelisks, all tucked neatly into deep green manicured grass.

"Trudy. Did we even have sex?"

"I know what you mean. I had the same thought. I was like so . . . out of my head that night and everything was so . . . *weird*, it was like it all *could* have been a dream."

"No. That's not what I'm saying. I'm saying . . ." I make a circle with my index and thumb and poke my finger repeatedly through it.

"Please stop that right now," she says.

So I do. I put my hands in my lap. Perhaps I'll never know.

She turns and reaches into her bag. "Here you go," she says, crying a little as she gives me the tiny amber pill bottle. And when I see that she's crying, I get a little choked up and the world goes shimmery from tears and then I'm full-on fucking bawling like a child. We both are. We move into each other's arms, our bodies shaking with sobs. A few minutes later, when we're finally calm and just lying back in the grass, our faces red and smeared, Trudy asks do I wanna smoke a bowl.

"No way. That'd push me right over the edge."

"Into what?"

"Depression. Anxiety. Paranoia. Insanity, basically. One of these graves."

"God, people are so weird," she says. "It's not drugs that make you that way, you know. It's the way we all already are."

I shift onto my elbow and look at her. "You said I might not have it."

"Yeah. I know." She smiles. "But I also said you might."

"I'm gonna kill myself," I say.

"Don't talk like that, okay? It's not funny."

"It's not supposed to be."

"And besides, what did I just tell you a minute ago?"

"That drugs are fun because they make us depressed."

"No. I said no more teenage death."

She pulls me very close. It feels good to be this close to someone and not be going crazy about how to undo their bra. "*Be a kid,*" she whispers, "*die later.*"

38

Am I still crying? Who knows what the fuck to call it. The fan is on, blowing right on me, but fails to soothe. The stereo is quiet, the Stratocaster in the corner against the wall, untouched. Everything previously a comfort now mocks me.

39

Almost crawled through the Hobart to try and get clean.

40

You are thirteen years old and walk the earth with an all-the-time ache throbbing in your precious nutters. The bikini brief phase. *Why?* The nocturnal emission. *Very great.* Your heart grinds away constantly, burns itself into ashes, always rematerializing. Choose your own adventure. It's winter in your bedroom. Make a gun with your finger and thumb. You aim at the silence, the permafrost, the diamond glint of the future.

The movie is *18 Again,* a switch comedy, the young and old switch bodies.

George Burns. Charlie Schlatter.

As before with Moore and Cameron. Reinhold and Savage.

But this movie. Now. The East-Towne 5.

Nora Reperton sitting next to you wearing a pink sweater and spotless pink Converse All-Stars and her fingernails are painted light pink. Her cheeks and lips glitter and shine in the flashing light from the screen. The coming attractions. The following preview has been approved for all audiences.

Her perfume smells like the vast rolling fields of heaven itself. It's Giorgio, she tells you. She and her mother both wear Giorgio. You want her to take you there. Her hand is warm in yours, ten fingers interlocked, sweat in the lifelines, thumbs moving slowly gently back and forth and oh the skin of her wrist.

Are we there yet? No.

Is it time yet? Yes.

Now. Do it now. Kiss her now. Take a breath. Bend and release.

The fires began with just a few tiny sparks way down deep in places in your heart you never knew existed and they're raging away now all out of control. This day, this moment. What was that poem? So much depends upon the last wild seconds before the kiss, when your veins are a million speedways pumping rocket-fuel blood.

You are standing in a bright field. You are listening to the earth, drawn back like a bow, tasting the stars, the honey, your mouth, the light. To touch her glittery cheek, to step through the screen and scream, the sins, the sinner, the night, the kiss . . .

Now.

There is nothing else but this moment, this movie, your hand in hers, do it now, kiss her now. No longer afraid to feel to fight to kick out against life to kiss to dream to dance to love to leave home to die to learn to fuck up fall down and forgive . . .

You tremble as you move toward her.

Nora.

Her mouth is there, slightly open. Your lips touch hers for a second, no, half a second, before you pull back, startled, shocked by the wetness. It was there, it was real, her mouth, but no, breathe in, be cool, try and keep it together . . .

And you are. And you do. You are so supercool that what you do is act like you only pulled away so you could spit out your gum. You remove the wad, about ten little pieces of Trident spearmint. It takes the rest of the century to fall to the floor.

Behind you someone coughs.

Something happens on screen. Mild laughter in the crowd.

Desire.

Is it time yet? Yes.

Nora is waiting. She looks at you and smiles. You clear your throat and lean over and kiss her and your tongues touch softly, beautifully, your fingers still entwined.

Now no one dies and everyone's happy. The world knows everlasting peace.

You have entered a state of permanent longing.

41

Out in the parking lot, almost done for the night, white smoke circles Wendell's head and hands like his soul escaping and he's humming softly the chorus to something it takes me a second to figure out is Guns N' Roses' "Patience." Dale is doing calisthenics, touching his toes for a ten count and every time he straightens up, he raises his arms up over his head and lets out a long relieved sigh. Across the way the Bayview sign reads *ALL U CAN EAT TACO TUES NECESSITY IS THE MOTH OF INVENTION*.

"The moth of invention," says Wendell. "What the fuck?"

Dale stretches, he chuckles. "You ever see that one *Simpsons*?"

"Nah, bro, I don't watch cartoons."

"Oh but it's so much more than that."

"Yeah? How do you figure?"

"Because, man, it's."

"Ain't it a buncha little animated people?"

"Yeah but you don't get it, dude. It's like . . . *satire*."

"Satire. Go the fuck back to college with that."

"Dude, I'm *in* college. Currently enrolled."

"Let me guess," I say. "The University of Life."

"You got it, Sweeney."

"And what kinda school is it, again?"

"A big old shitty one."

I roll up all the mats and I'm mopping the line when inspiration hits. That may be the one thing work is good for. Thinking about everything else except work. Most of the time this will lead you into the mind's dark corners. Yet every once in a while, if you're lucky, brilliance.

After Dale, Wendell and I punch out, we walk over to the Bayview and get to work on the sign, rearranging the letters, hiding behind the ship whenever a car comes. It's a serious business, all sweat and labored breathing, and we're silent and methodical. When we're done we step back and gaze at our creation, then crack the fuck up for a good five minutes. "Sweeney, I gotta hand it to you this time," says Dale.

Wendell says, "Let's go to my place, have some pops."

"You got a place?"

"Yeah. I call it Chateau Dale Fuck Off."

It turns out Wendell lives across the bay, just a five-minute walk away, right on the water, in a one-room, one-window shack with a cooler, TV, love seat and twin bed with no sheets. There is nothing in the cooler but ice and Bud tall boys.

"Wendell," I say, "are you from a movie?"

"Shut up and drink, Sweeney."

We each crack a tall boy and Dale proposes a toast.

"To the U of L," he says.

Wendell goes next. "To eating, shitting, working and dying," he says.

"All right," I say. "Here's to having not."

We knock cans and drink. The room is warm but the beer is so cold it seizes my temples and locks me up for a second before unleashing a terrific release, a giant hot and cold flower bursting into dramatic bloom, sped up, like on a nature show.

"We oughtta do more of that shit," Wendell says. "You know? Get into a little more trouble. Fuck more shit up. When

I was in my prime, boy, that's just about all we ever did was fuck shit up. Look at me now. It's sad. Living this respectable life."

"Say what? Respectable? You don't even have a refrigerator," Dale says.

"Yeah but I got a job, homes. And I go to that fucker every day, rain or shine. If I didn't, you best believe my PO would have my ass."

"PO? Dude, what the *fuck*?"

Wendell shrugs. "There's been some road bumps."

"No shit. What'd you go in for?"

"A buncha shit I did over the years so I wouldn't have to have a job."

"Dude, no. Let's back up here. Be specific."

"That's about as specific as I like to get."

"You got a record?"

"Yeah Einstein, I got a record. Then I got my shit together. Or I should say was *made* to get my shit together. And now look. Everything works out. I'm being *made* to live the American Dream. TV, job, a frosty pop after a hard day's work."

"Dude, wait a second."

"Yeah?"

"Tell me something."

"Yeah?"

"What's it all about, jail? What's that . . . whole scene like?"

"Why, you writin a book?"

"No. Just curious."

"You're awful quiet, Sweeney. Thought you'd be the life of the party."

"Just listening."

"So you're just curious and you're just listening. You all must be some smart motherfuckers. What's jail like? Good question. All I can say is sometimes . . . it's weird, sometimes I'll have some freaky thought when we're in the shit and Skip's going crazy and the waitresses and all. And I think of my goddamn nose-blow paycheck they pay me to stand around and do this. And I think *Man, I'd give anything to be back there.*"

"Back in jail?"

"Back where I at least knew where I stood. At least a little bit anyway."

He drains his second beer and burps, the last noise for a while. Dale grabs another tall boy and rolls the cold can across his neck. "Wendell, I'm telling you, dude, you gotta give *The Simpsons* another try."

"Maybe someday I will. Or maybe I'll just shove my balls back into my stomach and go back to fuckin kindergarten. Whattaya say?"

"Dude, you know that's not kind."

"Yeah but this is," letting out another tremendous burp.

My right knee pops as I stand. "Gotta shove off."

Wendell walks me the two inches to the door. "That was good earlier, man. Like I said, we gotta really fuck some more shit up."

"We will," I say, shaking the hand he offers. "For sure."

The door closes behind me. The only sounds on the walk back are the waves lapping in the bay and gravel crunching under my heels. I feel lonely and small, a piece of space dust floating through the endless galaxies. But I feel good too. It's good to be alone and hurting. Back in the Café parking lot, digging around for my keys, I look up the hill at the sign we made, lit in the darkness: *EAT ALL TITTIES OF INVENTION.*

42

No, Wendell, we won't.

I call Skip in the morning and tell him I can't come in. He says, "What are you saying, Sweeney, today or ever?" Still time to change my mind. I hear the kitchen in the pause, the bang of a pan in low-level static like holding a seashell to your ear.

"I'm saying ever."

"Good man, Sweeney. Thanks a lot. Fuck you." He slams down the phone.

Later I take a doxycycline, a shower, an aimless drive.

43

"All right," my mom says, clicking a fingernail on the counter. "You had a good run at the Café, a couple summers. It was time. Now you'll look for something else."

"Uh yeah," I say.

"Won't you?"

"No."

"Okay." She stretches the word to impossible lengths. "So what's the plan?"

"The plan?"

"Yeah. What's your strategy, what comes next?"

I tell her there is no plan, there is no strategy, there is no next.

"Well since you apparently have such a good handle on the situation and seem to have done quite a bit of thinking about, oh, little things like how you're gonna *live* at school in the fall, Vincent, why don't you go ahead and tell me what there *is* then?"

She stares at me the way only a disappointed mother can stare at her dipshit son, her only child, eyes searching with all the love and anger on earth for difficult answers to impossible questions that will never be asked as long as we live.

44

I bring a plate of Oreos out to the porch. Ed takes one, dunks it in his coffee and brings it up quickly to his mouth. I unscrew mine and scrape the cream with my teeth.

"Heard you retired," he says.

"No. I'm just taking a break."

Silence. He scratches his beard, sips his coffee. We stare into the shimmering pre-dusk brightness. The tall grass at the edge of the swamp waves in the wind. A couple of red-winged blackbirds swoop down and land on reeds and take flight again.

"It's summer," I say, as if I just now realized.

Ed repeats the word, then says, "Summer don't mean shit

after elementary school. It's like your birthday. Get to be my age, Vim, it's just another day."

"See now that's what I'm talking about. I don't want that."

"Nobody does." He shrugs. "Just kinda happens."

We finish the Oreos. Ed drinks his coffee down to the bottom then pitches the dregs over the side of the porch. "I been sittin here doin the math," he says. "Partner, I got more time in lunch hours than you got days worked."

"I know," I say softly. What else can I say?

"My old man, shit, he worked in the mill forty years, every damn day of the week, like me. Tell you what though. To this day, eighty years old, he could still go sunup to sundown. Yes sir, my old man'd put a day's work in tomorrow shame any motherfucker half his age. But you go ahead," he says, "you take your fuckin break."

45

Beholding the night sky and explosions there. Red, white and blue reflected off the water. Double-fisting sparklers and Keystone beers and screaming with laughter at every even remotely funny bullshit remark. Head racing with all the new trouble and fun. Our dreams are a pissing, a fart in the cosmos. Orange-fractured black. No wake. The spikes of each new blast sail sharply out before dulling to nothing. Beholding the houses along the shore and listen. The impotent pop of distant firecrackers. All of the brightness eventually fades. Beholding the beautiful asses.

46

The horror of this thing maybe living in my dick and blood. And AIDS? What if what if what if what if? So now I got a head swimming with grief and remembering.

47

Medicine. Vitamins. Kurt Cobain.

48

Still driving, waiting for the dawn. "Sleepwalk"—any version, the original by Santo and Johnny or the one by the Ventures playing now—is like a three-minute history of all the world's sadness, without any words to get in the way or fuck up the groove.

I stop at the Fourth Coast for more coffee. The NA and AA dudes are out in full effect, chain-smoking, playing checkers, chess and D&D, looking shell-shocked and kind. There's a few punks too, '70s throwbacks with black leather and liberty spikes and Exploited tattoos. I order a Walk the Plank—a large coffee mixed with three shots of espresso—and sit at the counter sifting through a pile of free weeklies. A few seats over is a bearded guy in more or less constant motion. He's wearing a safari hat and sunglasses. "Hey buddy," he says. "Yeah, you. You a shitter-hitter?"

"Am I a what now?"

"A shitter-hitter. You like the ass?"

I think for a moment as he rocks madly in his chair. "You know, I really do," I say. "I like the ass."

"My man." He grins and raises a hand for a high five. I sip the Walk the Plank till it cools, then guzzle it and order another. The clock over there over the bathroom door tells me it's almost three. There was a little part of my shirt I hadn't sweated through yet. Not anymore. Either that guy or me gets the gold medal for shaking to death.

SEARCHING FOR A LITTLE DEBBIE Fudge Round. The Ace-Hi party story is closed. All I can do is motor down Westnedge to the Meijer's Thrifty Acres in Portage. Every light is blinking yellow. It's all just strip malls out this way, feeding into the Crossroads, the really big mall, like rivers into the ocean. Ah but Meijer's. Glowing as brightly as a nuclear blast. The mechanical doors part, the AC hits like an answered prayer.

This place is so fucking huge it's a fucking biosphere. It's where you come if you want all in one trip oil for your car and socks and cold cuts and tennis shoes and potato chips and a *Yes, There Really Is a Kalamazoo!* T-shirt and a Stephen King book and Comet.

Or else it's four in the morning and you're driving around stoned on defeat and caffeine, squirting sweat like your pores are little microscopic turkey basters and all the nerves in your body are alive and screaming and you just want a fucking fudge round.

Walking toward the snack cakes.

Motherfuck the moon and New York City.

Now wait just a goddamn minute here. There's way too many of these bitches. This is worse than the cereal aisle.

Star Crunch?

No!

Oatmeal cream pie?

No!

Stick to the plan, baby. I pay for the fudge rounds and leave.

BACK ON THE HIGHWAY, I-94 headed west. Hit some way-out, nowhere exit, turn around, now it's east. We're really pushing the Subaru here, it's topping out around 70 mph and shit starts rattling. The steering wheel, the dashboard, the fudge rounds, my teeth.

These fudge rounds are good. I've killed about half the box.

I am driving straight at the sunrise. Another day with these hands and this face, what a pisser. I pull off in Battle Creek and park at a McDonald's and watch the early morning drive-thru breakfast crowd. Goddamn it, I want a sausage McMuffin too.

Heaven is fried.

I put the car in gear and drive away from the sunrise, back into the night.

YOU SHOULD NOT BE HERE BUT YOU ARE. You should feel guilty but you don't. You should turn around now and drive away and let it be something you do not regret because it did not happen, a bad idea that died before you did.

Chateau Acres burning in the clean morning sun.

33 Mangrove Way is way in the back, the next-to-last trailer before a drop-off and a low valley filled with pools of cotton-colored mist. I knock lightly at the screen door till a skinny bedhead kid in a Pistons back-to-back championships T-shirt answers.

"Hi. Good morning. Thought you were a Bulls fan."

"I am," he says, rubbing his face with both hands.

"Is your sister home?"

"Yeah. Who're you?"

"I'm, wow, just tell her it's Old Bull Lee."

A minute later Helene appears. She steps outside, blinking, wiping her eyes. "Vim?" she says, her voice low, full of sleep.

"Hey now. How are you?"

"Fine. What are you doing here?"

"I was just . . . you wanna get some breakfast or something?"

"You know what time it is, right?"

"Yes I do."

"It's seven in the morning."

"Yes I know."

Finally she wakes up enough to really see me. "Are you all right?" she says.

"Me? Yeah. I'm as right as the mail."

"Have you slept yet?"

"You mean ever in my life?"

"You gotta . . . you should go," she says.

"Why?"

"Because. My mom'll be home soon."

"I was kinda hoping we could talk."

"We can't."

"Just talk, is all I wanna do, I'm . . ."

I can't finish. I don't know what I want to say or even how to use my mouth to say it. I feel empty in the center. I feel floating. Helene is speaking with what looks from way back in here in my head like some degree of urgency. I tell her I only want to talk. I tell her hey you know it's funny what you said about god the murderer.

Funny because it's true.

She is saying something about what the hell am I saying. "Leave," she's saying, "you gotta trust me on this one and please . . ."

"In a minute," I tell her. I tell her all I want in the world this second is to talk.

I reach out to touch her and she moves back against the screen door. I only wanted to touch her arm. I know you know what I mean. I only wanted to talk.

"No Vim please you have to go away right now."

I just want to sit. I want a glass of water. I want to be home already in my bed sleeping and not have to drive there. I want to go down very deeply and dream and watch you dance and writhe.

A pale form materializes behind the screen to Helene's right. The door creaks open. It's Bixby Wheeler, wearing only sweatpants. There are deep red hickeys on his chest and stomach. "Vim?" he says. His voice too is weak with sleep.

"Yes Wheeler. It is I. How are you?"

"What are you doing here?" He looks at Helene. "What is he doing here?"

She shrugs sadly. "He got here a minute ago. I really don't know."

"Is everything okay?" Wheeler asks.

"No well I mean everything's all a little bit fucked up but I was . . . on my police scanner earlier it's a . . . new hobby of mine and lo and behold what do I suddenly hear about you now but a gas leak out this way. But things look . . . pretty okay."

A curtain flutters in one of the windows. Helene's brother. I turn away and Wheeler calls after me and then I'm falling and then I'm on the ground, looking up at the big blue sky. "Whoa. Watch out for that flower pot," I say. "There aren't even any fucking flowers in it. Did everybody have a good shit today?"

Wheeler bends over. "Come on, man, lemme help."

"No! Get off! Get away from me with your hickeys!"

"They're not hickeys. They're love marks," he says. And the thing about it that crushes my heart is he's being totally sincere.

Now I'm standing again, backing away and stumbling with my arms up and spread in the air like Dracula raising an invisible cape. "So. What's happening now?"

Helene opens the door. She steps inside and then back out. Her brother comes out and they all three look at me with weird dumb faces and I'm shouting:

"What's happening now!"

Wheeler rushes toward me, a finger pressed to his lips.

"Vim man come on keep it down."

I spin away and tumble backward onto the hood of my car. I scream:

"WHAT'S HAPPENING NOW!"

Wheeler's hands flutter all around, Helene is sideways in my vision, her brother looks at me like I'm something growing in a petri dish at school. I'm panting, coughing. Now there is no one, they all went inside. Still I'm screaming it over and over:

"WHAT'S HAPPENING NOW!"

Next door an old woman comes out of her trailer. She looks at me as she lights a long white-filtered cigarette. She's wearing some big flowing flowery nightgown thing. I roll off my car and fall back to the ground and stare up into her face.

"Hi," I say. "What's happening now?"

The woman blinks, takes a few puffs of her cigarette. "I don't know, Sonny. Suppose'n you tell me."

49

The old legend goes that he turned to my mother on that very last day on his way out the door and gestured toward wherever I was in the apartment and said to her *What will he think of me when he's old enough to know*? And in a way my whole life has been an answer to that question.

50

Heart as collapsed time, as dug-up grave, as simple machine. Heart as big black bugs bleed blue blood. Heart as MI frozen as seen from airplane, everything still and white and beautiful. Heart as the Day the Music Died. Heart as love being made, as fucking, as a pleasantly haunted house. Heart as a dim memory of a dark room in which you're molded wetasscracked into a beanbag chair, fumbling for wetness. Come hither. Heart as a cunt's supposed to smell like tuna. Heart as the star of the sea. Heart as a pussy in permanent bloom. Heart as doxycycline. Heart as waxwings, as a fudge round, as the phone rings once and then stops. Heart as throw your hands in the air, throw your art at the stars, stutter and stare. Heart as a Stratocaster. Heart as Twin Reverb. Heart as I heart you so much. Heart as all that we thought we knew in the world disappears into vapor. Heart as the rest of your life times the weight of the world squared.

51

An hour outside Kalamazoo the Quicksee signal begins to fade right in the middle of "Take a Letter, Maria," so I flip through the dial to WRKR, the Classic Rocker, whose signal reaches the very edges of space and time. We got a three-for from the Boss.

131 winds through Grand Rapids and beyond that it's nothing but farm stands, pine trees, mile markers and gas stations with a Subway or Taco Bell tucked in the back behind the racks of mesh hats and calling cards and trucker speed.

My Daughter And My $$$ Go To Michigan.

Just past Cadillac I stop at the Dairy King and order two chili-cheese dogs and a Reese's Blast. At the next picnic table is a family of fatties. I swear even their eyeballs are fat. One of the kids gives me a great big smile and the mom and dad notice so they smile too and when I finally give in and smile back, the kid busts out with the most gigantically pure laughter I've heard in forever.

"Who's that, Erroll," says the mom in a baby voice, "is that your new friend?"

The road again, climbing the state, crossing the 45th Parallel, halfway between freezing and hell. At some point even the Rocker dropped out and I've been listening to static and didn't even realize.

My Son Is An Honor Roll Student at Martinville Middle School.

Off to my left tiny slivers of Lake Michigan drop in and out of view before it fully explodes into a gorgeous endless blue, as if it covered the whole rest of the world. I've tried to tell people who've never seen it and don't understand that no, you really can't see the other side.

There are strip malls now on the outskirts of Petoskey, on either side of the road into town, a valley of dollar stores, a Sam's Club, more fast-food joints, a gleaming new Best Buy. None of this shit existed last year. It must have been airlifted in.

I Owe I Owe It's Off To Work I Go.

Uncle Bro lives alone in a small green house on Wachtel St with guitars in every room, even the bathroom. The door is unlocked and there's a note on the table.

WELCOME VIM
GRAB A BEER.

52

The Depot Tavern is a dark place with a peanut-shell floor. One room is the bar, the other's the dining room. Bro and I are in the dining room, sitting in the very last booth. The tabletop is heavy with a carved-out history and I run my hand slowly over the big worn grooves, all the names, dates, loves and fuck yous. The waitress smiles when I order a white Russian and doesn't ask to see i.d.

"Interesting choice," Bro says.

"They're good, man. They taste like candy."

"I know what they taste like. Who turned you on to that shit?"

"Jake did."

"Really? I'm surprised. I figured him for more of a hard stuff–type guy."

"Vodka's hard."

"Not when you drink it with Hershey's syrup and milk."

"All right so if you see the waitress, flag her down. I'll change my order."

"To what, a cosmo? White wine spritzer?"

"No. Scotch. A nice single-malt."

"A mudslide, maybe? Something served in a pineapple with faggot umbrellas?"

"Fuck you. I'm gonna see if they have moonshine here. Pure grain alcohol."

The waitress returns with my white Russian and his Miller High Life. We talk and I tell him everything. He nods, he knows. Another round. He tells me he's seeing a new girl and it finally feels right this time. He always had a bunch, played the field etc. For a long time, in Kalamazoo, he had a serious girlfriend. They were living together, engaged forever. But rock and roll, man, it's tough on commitment.

Where were you?

Babe you know I had a gig last night.

Yeah I know you had a gig till one o'clock. *One.* It's six in the morning.

I went and played guitar with Silas afterward I told you . . .

For five straight hours you played guitar with Silas? *Five straight hours?*

Babe please you're being crazy . . .

Show me your hands let me see your fingers!

Jesus . . .

They better just be bleeding goddamn stumps . . .

Till finally she couldn't take it. She gave up and left. Larissa was her name. The new girl is Cherie and she can hang, apparently. She knows about music and makes a killer baked good. She's got her hooks in deep. He claws at his heart, demonstrating what this means. "She made me a new man," he says.

53

In the dream my father appears holding a guitar and then vanishes. Random traces of Helene, her smell, her voice. She says *I thought you said you didn't want to fuck me.* I say *Did I say that? Because that's not true, I totally want to fuck you.*

54

Takes a second to remember where I am. Uncle Bro's basement, on a twin bed in the corner. A tiny fan clipped to the cracked wood paneling blows cool mildewed air over me. The darkness down here is complete. The clock says after two but a.m. or p.m.?

55

Under a tree under a canopy of stars. Every house along Wachtel has a porch light on with thick flurries of bugs circling the dim light around the fixture. In the lawn next door a broken Big Wheel lies on its side in the overgrown grass. I walk to the end of the block and take a left and there's Dawn Donuts, all raging fluorescence inside. The only other person is a guy wearing a flannel with the sleeves cut off and a hat with an American flag over the words *Burn This One, Asshole*. A WWF pinball machine spits out blips and urgent calls to action.

Get over here!

Think you got what it takes HUH?

The woman who comes through the swinging double doors weighs easily three hundred pounds. But what really gets me is the five o'clock shadow all down her neck. It's so thick and bristly I kind of want to reach out and scratch it. Instead I order a black forest, a toasted coconut and a large coffee. It's the kind of coffee I'm learning to love, scorched so bad it's almost sweet tasting. I sit at the counter and listen to the radio on a shelf above the coffee maker and suddenly I'm misty. If there's one song that gets me sobbing for the old days, it's "Broken Wings." The moody keyboard line. The stark black-and-white video. A minute later the flannel guy gets up from his booth and sits right next to me. "Nelson Maddox," he says, extending a hand.

"Good for you."

"Oh I see. A hardass."

"Not really."

"Good. It's way too late in the night for that shit. What's your name?"

"Darby Crash." We shake.

"Cool to meet you, Darby. Where do you hail from?"

"Day-twah."

"Wow. Where's that?"

"Michigan. Detroit."

"Oh shit," he laughs, "I see. From the French."

"That's right. The Paris of the Midwest."

"If that's the case, looks like Paris burned down about thirty fuckin years ago."

"Things are good there now."

"That so? I see it on TV sometimes. Don't look so good to me. Whattaya do over there, if you don't mind me asking?"

"I'm in rock and roll."

"No shit? You famous?"

"Not yet."

"Well hey man, chin up, you just gotta keep at it!"

"Maybe. But you know, Nelson, fame isn't always the ultimate goal."

"Really? What's the goal then? Money? Dope? Pussy? What?"

"There is that element, for sure."

"What other elements are there, do you suppose?"

"Well. Art," I say.

"Come again?" says Nelson, putting a finger to his ear.

"There's the art of it. Creating something beautiful and lasting."

"Tell me, Darby, are you on dope now?"

"No. Just coffee and doughnuts."

"So you're shitting me then?"

"Nope. Crappin you negative."

"The art of rock and roll," he says. He offers me a cigarette then lights one for himself. Prince's "1999" comes on.

"Like this one," I say, "this one touches on something pretty deep."

"Such as?"

"Millennial anxiety. Sex. Death. The end of pretty much everything. Listen, here's the line. Wait. Here it comes. Right here. Did you hear that?"

"Something about I was dreaming and I spoke this?"

"No, after that. 'Life is just a party and parties weren't meant to last.'"

"Life's a *party*? Fuck that. Where's the art? My life's no party."

"Yeah but it's one of those scary truths. Prince is saying we're all gonna die."

"Is that really all that deep, though, Darby? To sing about how we're all gonna die? Isn't that just like," he shrugs, "no shit, motherfucker, go get a job."

"Nelson, you don't got a job." It's the Bearded Lady. She came out in time to hear this last bit.

"I'm *looking*," says Nelson. "It's the fucking *economy*."

"Yeah. The economy. Gimme a cigarette."

Beardo and Nelson chain-smoke a while. Her real name's Althea. She wears a red smock and her hands are white with flour. Every time she raises the cigarette to her face she leaves a little trace on her upper lip. A long block of commercials fades into John Cougar Mellencamp. "Now this is more my speed," Nelson says.

"Cougar's good," I say.

"These are the songs for my philosophies. Not life's a party. Althea, crank that, will ya." She turns the radio up loud and when the chorus comes on we all sing along.

> *Ain't that America, for you and me*
> *Ain't that America, something to see, baby*

Grab On to Me Tightly as if I Knew the Way

Then the instrumental section, the breakdown, the quiet part, the freak-out *VACATION DOWN AT THE GULF OF MEXICO!* part, back into the chorus a bunch of times, and then the song ends. "Fuckin A," says Nelson, nodding in approval.

"Why don'tcha fuck an O," Althea says. "They're easier."

56

Cherie might even be a hair taller than Bro. Her legs are a wonder, long and tan with perfect muscle tone. And I'm not even a leg man. Give me great big globes and ass. She was married once, she tells me, for about ten minutes. "It was a high school sweetheart thing. Except in the end it turned out to be not so sweet."

"You were too young," Bro says.

"Nah. Just too stupid. Plenty of people get married young and stay married."

"No one I know," he says.

"You've just been running with the wrong crowd, babe."

"I know people who got married young and stayed married and they're miserable now and wanna bash each other's brains in. Does that count?"

"Oh yeah. As long as you respect that sacred bond."

"Like my parents," I say.

"Your folks are still married?"

"Not the original set, no."

"Yeah but in your case you're better off," Bro says. "Ed's a stand-up guy."

"Who's Ed?"

"My stepdad."

"Stepdads. That's a tough road," Cherie says. "I had one once. He was such a huge bastard. I swear, half the time, the look on his face, it was like he didn't know whether he wanted to beat me up or feel me up or what."

"Jesus," Bro says, "doesn't anything end happy with you?"

"You never know. Maybe this," she says. She gives him one of the lovers' looks I hate so much only this time I don't mind. Cherie grows prettier with conversation. She and Bro are loosely hugging and I reach for another cookie, my fifth.

"Now about these," I say, holding up the cookie, chocolate chip and coconut. Cherie smiles. It's a wonderful warm smile. Great. Is there anyone I don't fall in love with? "The coconut brings everything into a, into quite a clear focus."

57

Walking down Mitchell St in the middle of the day, all the Fudgies out and about. The dads have fanny packs with their big fat guts hanging over. As far as the mothers, well, let me just say it's an atrocity what happens to a woman's ass in middle age. But I raise my Slurpee in a toast to your fantastical daughters, all white capris and golden limbs and canvas boat shoes. Pure all-American beaver on parade.

58

Everyone roaming the halls in a panic like *This is the end of the world!* Penny Benjamin stops me at the Coke machine, all melodramatic, almost in tears, and says: "Vim it's happening, they're bombing Baghdad."

And I'm like: "Okay but this machine just swallowed my last fucking buck."

But she looks so beautiful in the Coke machine glow, red reflecting off her blue eyes and blond hair and white T-shirt, tucked in, and she's all put together and perfect except for the confusion and sadness pouring out of her like water.

Someone in the AV room hooked up a TV in the hallway

and a few of us stand around watching strange little flashes flicker on a black screen.

Mr Punt, my history teacher, walks by, clucking his tongue. What the hell's that about? That motherfucker has a poster of Garfield on his classroom wall with Garfield with books all tied to his feet saying *I'm Learning by Osmosis*.

I bust out laughing. I've been waiting my whole life for Garfield to make me laugh and it's now. But mine is the only laughter anywhere.

Someone says: "What's so funny, Sweeney? Huh?"

I say: "Garfield, man."

Someone else says: "Can it, Sweeney."

I say: "I'm flipping you off by osmosis."

Someone else says: "Fuck it. I'd like to blow up Saddam."

I say: "USA all the way! Hoo hoo hoo!"

Someone says: "Sweeney, get lost."

So I get lost. Weirdness everywhere. Outside it's crazy cold. The light's already failing. All the Christmas decorations are still taped up in the windowed hall by the office and I feel a draft as I walk through, cold in just a T-shirt.

I'm wearing a black shirt that says *Death to the Pixies*.

I stop by the White Room and linger in the doorway and say hey to Mitchell Bucket, the young wingnut Christian who supervises in-school suspension. There's a couple kids in there at the desks with dividers running up the sides so they can't see anything, reading ancient issues of *Popular Mechanics*. I have spent many days in the White Room and the bad part is self-evident but the good part is the bathroom down a narrow hallway in the back, the only bathroom in the whole school with a locking door for privacy in shitting. Otherwise it's hold it and wait till after four. "So Mitchell," I say, "looks like your guy's got the goods to go to war."

Mitchell is super young Republican, almost like out of a sitcom. I was in the White Room actually on election day and remember saying I wished Dukakis would win. Mitchell looked at me sadly and said: "I'm glad the day's over and you're about to leave this room."

But I wasn't sweating it. The dude's got a Jesus fish on his Toyota.

He says: "Mr Sweeney, don't you have a class to be at?"

I say: "You know Mitchell, you should never end sentences in prepositions."

"Oh really? Well maybe you'd like to sit and tell me about it a while."

"Are you trying to trick me, Mitchell? You are, aren't you? I'm on to you, pal."

"Get to class, Mr Sweeney."

"All right, Mitchell. Thanks for the pep talk, old sport."

"Anytime. And hey, I'm sure I'll see you in here soon."

I wander past the Devil's Den, the student commons, down the art hall, and take a right. A minute later I'm at the gym. It's eerie, there's no one around, it's totally silent. Usually you can hear the ball-bounce and whistle of good clean phys. ed. Could be Mr Van Ward's planning hour. But what the fuck does he plan?

1) *Sit around for a while, wait for students to change.*

2) *Take attendance.*

3) *Hand out basketballs and then just kinda hang out and watch.*

Lather, rinse, repeat.

I'm standing at the trophy case looking at pictures of old

crazy '70s-looking Gull Lake champion sports stars when I hear someone behind me.

"Penny?" I say.

"Hey Vim."

She must have been really crying for real. Her pretty face is swollen and red. Her hair is unbrushed with a strand stuck in the corner of her mouth. She moves it away. Again she says my name. She says it so softly she could almost be pleading for something. And she looks, wow, she looks so goddamn sad. I've never seen anyone my age look so sad and crushed. At least not about world events.

I say: "Penny, is this . . . I mean are you bummed out because of the war?"

She says: "Aren't you scared?"

I shrug. I don't say anything.

She says: "Please tell me you're scared. You've gotta be. You've *gotta* be."

"Why," I say, "why do I *gotta* be?"

"Because," she says, "they're killing people, they're . . ."

"Look. Everything's gonna be okay," I say. "Like the um, the Bob Marley song."

She puts her face in her hands and cries soundlessly.

"Penny," I say. I go toward her. I hold my arms up to hug her and then stop. Where the hell is everyone? I swear if a frog farted out in the grass we'd hear it.

And then she walks toward me and *she* hugs *me*. Oh my fuck. She holds me tightly around the neck and she's warm with her tits pressed against me, crying softly, her body shuddering, oh my fuck. I've never really held a girl before, especially not like this, in a time of sadness and grief.

Grab On to Me Tightly as if I Knew the Way

My mind fires off a series of thoughts that have nothing to do with comforting Penny in her time of sadness and grief.

Oh no, oh no, oh no.

Can she feel my raging boner? She must.

I stand like a statue, hardly breathing, staring through the trophy case glass at the wrestlers, moving my hand slowly over Penny's back. I feel her bra strap, oh no. She says something I can't hear. She sniffles. Then she looks up at me, right in my eyes.

She says: "What are the Pixies?"

I don't reply.

She says: "Vim?"

Again I say nothing.

"What's your T-shirt mean?" she says.

"It's . . . just a band."

"Oh. So you never answered my other question."

"What other question?"

"Are you scared?"

We're still holding each other. I should be in Earth Science right now, watching the cars out on M-89. But no matter what happens, whatever they do to me, if they stick me in the White Room for the rest of my life, it was worth it. I'd die for this moment.

"Well I'll tell you something, Penny, that's . . . boy, is that ever complicated."

"You're not alone," she says.

I look at her and smile, the kind of knowing half smile I used to flash all the time back in the day, after *Raiders* came out and I'd be imitating Indiana Jones. "Sure I am," I say.

After she leaves I touch my shirt, damp with her tears. I lick my fingers and I swear I can taste her pain. I see into her future and the future of the universe too and there's a fake god smiling through broken teeth down from a burning sky.

I get lost again. Eventually the bell rings.

59

Silence. And then after the silence, "Hey Darby."

"Yeah?"

"You wanna tell me a secret?"

"What do you mean?"

"A secret. One of yours. Could be anything. Go ahead, man. Unload."

"Nelson, what the fuck are you talking about now?"

"Just one of the things I do, man. It's my public service."

He shifts on the stool, reaches into his wallet and slaps a laminated business card down on the counter:

N. MADDOX
KEEPER OF SECRETS
"NO SECRET TO SMALL"

I turn it over in my hands. The plastic is grimy and worn, as if turned over by a thousand hands before mine. "Anyway," he says. "Free of charge. And I don't tell a soul. But no pressure though. Let's not fuckin overthink this. You seem like an overthinker."

"I do?"

"Oh for sure. Looking for meanings in rock songs and shit."

Then there's a pause as he stares into his coffee cup and I keep playing with the card. "So you heard a lot of secrets in your day or what?"

"More secrets up here, man," tapping his head, "than they got stars in the sky."

I put the card back on the counter. "Nelson, you're forgetting something."

"What's that?"

"I don't even *know* you."

"Hey true enough. You don't know me from fuckin Adam. Or Eve, for that matter. But Darby, there exists in this world a little thing I like to call trust. And from time to time—not all the time, god knows, hardly ever, really—but once in a blue moon, well, you just gotta put your trust in people. Without trust, man, I shudder to think."

60

I've heard the story many times, from my mom and from Ed, who wasn't even there but who tells it like he was and gets a huge kick out of it. But as Bro drains his beer and launches into it again I'm listening with brand-new ears. "First time I meet Joe Sweeney," he says, "he comes over to the folks' for a big Sunday dinner. Tall as a motherfucker. Skinny. Big hornrims.

Tight white turtleneck. Duke and I look at each other like *Who the fuck's this?*"

"Duke?" from Cherie, lying on the couch, right hand resting what's left of her drink on her stomach.

"My brother. We're the youngest, man, the black sheep. We did so many drugs back then you could have powered a third world country. It was funny actually, we had a little grow in our mom's garden, just a few plants. No one ever knew. The Commander, he had no clue what a pot plant looked like. A gin bottle, sure. Whiskey, vodka, wine, no problem. And that's what old Joe Sweeney walked into. His new girlfriend's crazy alcoholic dad and her high-strung mom and two stoned brothers. I kind of feel bad for the guy, looking back."

"Weird to think of my mom as someone's girlfriend," I say.

Cherie says, "Why? She's still a girl, you know. Just 'cause we grow up and our hair turns gray, it doesn't mean we stop being girls. Same way no matter how old you get, you'll always be a boy. Like your uncle. Look at him. Still just a boy."

Bro smiles briefly. He looks down at his empty High Life bottle, works back a corner of the label and then reapplies it, smoothing it out with his thumb. "Right away Joe Sweeney goes to work," he says, "talking to the Commander about, you know, naval history and World War Two and obscure battles and shit."

"That's his thing, man. War histories, the Civil War."

"Which is weird, don't you think, because he seems like such a pussy otherwise. But the Commander was fucking eating it up, slapping him on the back, laughing at all his jokes. That's the thing about *my* dad. He treated his own kids, his own flesh and blood, like total shit. But if you're a stranger, an outsider, someone else's kid, a boyfriend or girlfriend, well then hey, let's all have a beer and be friends. To this day, he's still nicer to the waiter at Bill Knapp's than he's ever been to me or your mom or any of us. But give old JS credit. My mom dug him too. I mean he'd fucking, he'd read all the books, man, he had the intellectual shit down *pat*. And he smiled a lot. None of us really smiled. I wanted to. But a lotta the time I was too pissed off or too stoned or both. Plus he'd been in the army, so that was big shit. Even though obviously I could have kicked his ass with all four limbs tied together, the fact that he'd been in the army got him points in the Commander's book. He never saw combat but so what. I guess just being there you learn discipline and I don't know, all that other bullshit. I mean, one day the Commander comes to me and he's fucking yelling about something and he gets all up in my face, you know, so close I can smell his breath and he's spraying all his spit all over me and poking me in the chest and he says *It's just too goddamn bad you're too young to go fight. If you were old enough I'd drag your ass downtown and fucking volunteer you myself.* So that's who we're dealing with here. A guy who wants to send his own kids to Vietnam. So Duke and I, just before dinner we go to the basement and burn a huge reefer and get high as a motherfucker, man, I mean like . . . drooling stoned. And we get hungry. And it's *powerful*. I'm fucking crawling out of my skin with the force of this hunger. But I know it's gonna be all right because my mom's making spaghetti, a big giant pot of it, which is like, one of her signature dishes. We're down there eating our fingernails, Duke and I, waiting for the word. Finally it comes. We go upstairs and sit at the table and right in the middle's the dish. The lid comes off. I wanna dive in the spaghetti and live in it the rest of my life. No. Joe Sweeney, being the guest, gets first crack. Someone slides it over and the motherfucker starts . . . *piling* it on, he *heaps it on* till there's a little mountain almost spilling over the side of his plate. I'm watching this happen in utter horror. By the time it comes around to me, there's *barely* enough for a kid-sized portion. Even Duke, man, he got his. I'm the only one suffering. And I'm seething, seeing red, just . . . I'm enraged. But what still fucking gets me after all this time, twenty years later, Joe Sweeney barely touches the food on his plate, barely even fucking glances at it. I finish my kid portion in about a minute, look over. Joe Sweeney's talking, laughing, drinking wine, making jokes, holding forth, basically doing everything except *eating*. Now and then he'll move the food around, play with it, make a little pile, smush it with his fork, take a little bite or two, just for show. End of the meal, my mom says *Finished, Joe? Oh yes, thank you, that was delicious,* he says. And she takes his plate into the kitchen and scrapes his big mountain of spaghetti off into the garbage. God I wanted to grab him by his turtleneck and yell *What the fuck's wrong with you, Fuck-eye? That was my spaghetti.*"

"Babe," Cherie's laughing, "you're insane," she says.

"How do you figure?"

"Because it was just damn *spaghetti*."

"All right, so apparently you don't understand."

"Hey man, I understand."

"See? Vim's the only one who gets me."

I move up on the floor into a sitting position. "Kinda wish you would've done it though."

"What?"

"Grabbed the old turtleneck and given the dude a good

shaking. Told him to get in the wind. Who knows, you might've saved me some trouble that way."

"How's that?"

"Well for one thing I might never have been born."

"Good point," Bro says, nodding thoughtfully. After a minute he stands and in the same motion lobs the empty bottle, now without a label, and I reach up and catch it instinctively. "But if you were never born who'd be going to the store right now to get more beer?"

61

A big concert at an outdoor stadium. R.E.M. plays an hour-long version of "96 Tears," the keyboard riff on a constant loop, driving me crazy. Michael Stipe touches my hand. He says *Sing with me, Vim.* So we sing "The Boxer." A sea of hands reaches toward me. Stipe's breath is hot against my face, his voice like I've heard in interviews, soft, Southern, vaguely lispy. He tells me I'm like the Beatles at Shea. Then I look back at the crowd but there's no one. I'm trying to punch but can't make a fist. I hit the door, the wall, whatever. I'm burning with anger even in dreams as my deathbed words echo back: *I am leaving I am leaving but the fighter still remains.*

62

Cherie works at a real estate office on Mitchell St and we meet for lunch at the Depot Tavern. Weird to be in here in the middle of a bright summer day. She lights a cigarette, waves at the smoke and says, "Don't tell your uncle. I'm quitting."

We order food, we talk. I tell her about Wheeler and Helene.

"That's pretty complicated," she says. "What are you gonna do?"

"I don't know. That's kind of why I'm up here."

"Well you can't stay in Petoskey forever. Why would you want to?"

"I like it up here. It's pretty. It's far away from all the bad shit."

"Yeah but stuff has a way of catching up with you. You leave all your friends and the girl and your parents and sooner or later they all catch up with you. They may not be physically beating down your door but for sure they're in here."

She taps the center of her chest. I shudder slightly.

"I could join Bro's band," I say.

"You don't wanna do that."

"I don't?"

"Hell no. Not unless you wanna play the same songs in the same order every weekend for the rest of your life."

"Bro digs it. It pays the bills."

"I think he digs it and he doesn't, to be honest with you. He and I haven't talked much about it but a part of me thinks he always wanted to get his own thing going and do his own music. And it's not too late for that. But I'm sure it's harder now than it was ten years ago. Like you said, it pays the bills. Anyway," she says, finishing her chicken sandwich. "Back to you. Let's think about what you're gonna do when you roll back into town." She lights another cigarette.

"I thought I might propose."

"I'd hold off on that if I were you."

"Okay. But shouldn't I at least tell her I love her?"

"Are you totally sure you do?"

"What do you think, I'm some amateur? On second thought, don't answer that."

"What do you love about her?"

"I don't know. I think it's . . . I don't know. Talking about that stuff tends to ruin it, don't you think? Makes it seem kinda corny."

"Oh?"

"Yeah. It's tough to talk about love and not sound like a greeting card."

"Pretend I didn't say love then. Tell me what you *like* about her."

"She's got these scars all over her arms. Self-inflicted."

"*That's* what you like about her?"

"No but isn't it weird?"

"No. I've met a hundred girls like that, a thousand. I've also met the dudes like you that wanna save all the beautiful, damaged, fucked-up girls of the world."

The waitress comes by and I order a white Russian.

"Drinking midday," Cherie says, "not a good sign."

"It's mostly just cream."

She lights yet another cigarette and crushes it out half-smoked, exhaling out of the side of her mouth. "Last one," she says. "I gotta get back in a minute."

"Right. Back to real estate, your true passion."

"Don't joke about that," she says. "And don't ever joke about love."

"Why not?"

"Because. Joking about that stuff'll come back to haunt you."

The drink arrives and sits on the table before me, untouched. "What if I want to be haunted?" I say.

63

I want you like this, I swear I do, and I want you to peel back the layers of time and show me the past and smack me around but in a playful way like lovers and hit me again, punch, reach out and claw, stick your fingers in my mouth, peel back the layers of my face to the person I am or whoever I want to be and punch me, baby, with hands like pale birds diving away from earthworm scars and your eyes, holy shit, your eyes lit up like groovy blue storms, everything electric, your heart beating into your tongue and your tongue inside my mouth and speak to me please using only your tongue, write the words in my mouth with it, I want you I swear to peel back the sky and show me all that's come before us and who we will be and all we will inevitably eventually lose.

64

I'm playing rhythm on his old Gretch hollow body, he's playing lead on a brand-new Martin. Watching his fingers on the frets is a miracle sometimes, so fast and clean. He's such a clean player. Every note is deliberate, like a pre-awful Clapton. Cherie taps her foot, she drinks her drink, eyes closed. Bro does this jazzy-sounding octave run up the neck, higher and higher, and his face contorts till it's nearly a grimace, then he takes it back down again and the pattern dissolves and the song is over. The last notes ring out and linger in the room. "I love that one," Cherie says. Her eyes are still closed.

"To me those chords sounded like northern California," he says, "that same sort of vibe, the coast, a place I'd never even been to at the time. So I called it 'Big Sur.' Ever heard of it? Me either. I only knew it from the title of a Kerouac book."

I show him the chords to "I'm Only Sleeping," the last song I actually bothered to sit down and figure out. We put on *Revolver* and play along but something about the bridge keeps throwing us so Bro gets down and kneels in front of the speaker, as close to the music as he can possibly get. He lifts the needle on the record player and backs it up, lifts the needle and backs it up. He reaches out and touches the speaker. "That's good, Lennon," he says, as if John Lennon were in the next chair. Then he picks up a guitar and plays the bridge perfectly. Then he shows it to me.

•   •   •

"THIS IS YOU."

"What?"

"Listen."

"Why? Who's."

"You. Listen."

Lines form on my face and hands lines form from the ups and downs I'm in the middle without any plans I'm a boy and I'm a man I'm eighteen and I don't know what I want.

"First of all, I'm seventeen. Second, who is this?"

"Alice Cooper."

"Ooh I *love* Alice Cooper," Cherie says.

"Well that's saying a hell of a lot, since you also *love* Paul McCartney."

"Fuck you, honey. Alice is the man."

"Are you guys for real? What about that song he did for the Jason movie, *Friday the 13th* part fifty or whatever. That was some pretty rock-bottom shit."

"Six. It was part six. *Jason Lives.* And that was all about a paycheck. This here, this is all about the *rock*. And hey, don't judge. You're washing dishes over there."

"Not anymore. I told you. I quit. I'm free."

Bro had been taking a swig when I said this and he spits beer in a big spray and chokes for a second and then starts laughing. He pounds his chest, takes another swig. "Sorry," he says and then starts laughing again.

"What the fuck?" I say.

"Nothing. Sorry."

Cherie looks over, grinning.

"You are," he says, "you're free."

And it's one of those things. A minute later we're all laughing. I fall on the floor and grab at Cherie, who wipes at the tears running down her cheeks. Bro's head is back and his mouth is wide open but he's not even making any sound anymore. "I'm free," I say again. We crack up some more. The record skips. We are living inside this laughter. It's as big as the house, bigger. It's so big I run outside into the quiet street.

65

Think I'll take a rest right . . . *here*. Ah. Lying facedown in the sand on Mt McSauba Beach. A thousand years later I roll over and sit up. Across the inlet is a factory with little twinkling green and red lights. Someone said they make cement there. The beach is dotted with bonfires, distant voices, tiny laughter. I dig my fingers into the sand and pull up cool handfuls. Two shadows turn into people, a guy and a girl, headed my way.

"Hello pals," I say.

"Hey there," from the male, "we're looking for Tony Patch."

"I am not him."

"No shit, Shakespeare. But is he around down the beach there?"

"Not to my knowledge, which I have to admit is limited."

"Okay, good enough. What the hell are you doing?"

"Not much. Contemplating suicide."

"Whoa. That's heavy. You better get off your ass and come with us."

"Do I have to?"

"Yes."

I squint up at the girl. "Why don't you speak, honey?"

"Why don't *you*?" she says.

"Well. I am."

"Enough chitchat," says the dude. "Let's move."

We walk in silence. Gradually we come upon a gathering. I see my new friends clearly in the firelight. No one here has heard of Tony Patch. Or no wait, someone has but he's maybe down that way? Pointing out into the darkness. We walk on.

"When I find that motherfucker," says the guy.

"Yeah, what?" I say.

"Nothing." He laughs. "Good times."

"So why do you wanna off yourself?" says the girl.

"Why do *you*?"

"Touché. But I don't."

"Me either. Not anymore. You saved me."

"Wow. I never saved anyone before. This is exciting."

Our arms brush together, the backs of our hands.

"Wait'll you meet good old T Patch," the guy says. "Good times."

"Good times and great oldies," I say.

But it's the same deal at the next stop and the next one after that. We walk from fire to fire and everyone's like: Tony Patch? Yeah I don't really know the dude but I'm pretty sure he's around here somewhere, a friend of a friend told me etc.

"Man oh man oh man. When I find that motherfucker."

"Come on, you gotta tell me," I say. "What's gonna happen? I'm dying to know."

"Look man, I wish you wouldn't talk like that, considering your current state of mind and all. I'm here for you. Rachel and I both are."

Finally our quest is temporarily derailed. Turns out the guy knows some people here and we stop. A huge fire, the biggest I've seen, thick black smoke going upward. I'm down at the water again with Rachel. "I like you," she says.

"Now how could you possibly know that?"

"Because. I can tell. You're beautiful."

"Beautiful? Is that a joke?" I look around. "Am I on fucking *Candid Camera*?"

"No. What's wrong with that? Don't you think you're beautiful?"

I laugh for about five minutes and finally eke out a no. She's closer to me now and it's getting sexier. I point behind me and say, "What about homes?"

"Who?"

"Your boyfriend."

"Who, Maurice? He's not my boyfriend. I don't really have boyfriends. I'm more about *experience*. I don't need to be all wrapped up in someone else's trip."

"I see. Their trip. What decade do you live in again?"

"This one. Experience never goes out of style."

"Good point. Will you please take off your shirt now, please?"

"You're so bold. I had no idea. You looked so helpless there in the sand."

Shaking my head. "It's all a big fucking, what's the word, façade."

"Which, bold or helpless?"

"Both of them."

Nothing matters, not the endless, heaven-high fire behind us or the truth beneath those waves or this chick's tongue. I started it. Use me, take me with you to hell or your mother's house. We scale the dune and get in her car and hit the winding back roads of Charlevoix. "We're gonna have to be quiet," she says.

"Why are you doing this?" I say a few minutes later.

"Because you asked me," Rachel says, "because you said please twice."

It's a tiny perfect house in a clearing in some thick woods. A white dog greets us as we walk in the door and follows us down the hall, into the room. "Hey Lucky." She scratches Lucky's ears and kisses Lucky's nose. Then she kisses me, pulls me by my shirt down to the floor. "My parents'll hear if we're on the bed," she whispers.

Lucky lies near us, basically just being a dog.

As we're kissing and rubbing she reaches for the pecker, her strange warm fingers on my belly. The levels shoot into the red and a switch flips. Cold fear spills in and floods the system. I put my hand on hers to stop it from going further.

"Isn't this what you wanted?" she says.

"It was. Not anymore." Now just who the fuck is using my voice here?

"Oh. Well. What do you want then?"

"Only this," I say, hugging her. She hugs me back. I put my head on her chest, on her breasts. Lucky gets up and stands over us and I feel the warm dog breath. I reach up and stroke the fur. "What do you wanna be when you grow up?" Rachel says.

"Someone else," I say. "How about you?"

"My mother's a nurse. I definitely don't wanna be that."

"What then?"

"Something where you get to travel, like a flight attendant."

"You're not afraid to fly?"

"No," she laughs. "Are you?"

"Yes."

"Is there anything you're not afraid of?"

We lie together on the floor drifting in and out of sleep till the light at the window changes. In another room a clock radio comes on and Rachel makes me get under the bed. Good move. About ten minutes later the door opens slowly and her father walks in. I can tell from the Caterpillar work boots. "Hey Lucky, hey girl."

Rachel shifts on the bed and releases a long theatrical sigh. "Hi Daddy."

"Hey," he whispers, "just lettin Lucky out. Go back to sleep."

"Is Mom going in today?"

"Yeah but not for a while yet. We'll see ya."

Again with the big fake yawn. "Okay," she says. The door closes.

Not for a while yet?

Rachel gets out of bed and leaves the room. I hear her voice dimly, addressing her mother. A car starts out front and then a shower turns on somewhere. A couple of cupboards slam and then Rachel's back. She slips a Pop-tart under the bed. "Sorry," she whispers. "It's just till my mom leaves. Close your eyes maybe, try and sleep."

Maple and brown sugar, my favorite flavor Pop-tart. There

are worse things. At least the room smells good, even down here among the old bags and shoeboxes. Rachel begins snoring gently above me. I close my eyes and sleep and dream.

66

"I never remember my dreams but this one Joe Sweeney was in, which is strange. I don't remember my dreams usually, I don't know, I mean I'm sure I have but I don't know if I ever dreamt about him before. I must have, right? If I did, it must have been years ago, right around the time we split up. We were still in Jackson then and you were."

"Mom, okay, get on with it."

"All right so anyway so he's standing outside on the front porch and it's cold out, below zero, and it starts snowing, and he's just . . . standing there. And the snow starts piling up on his shoulders and on the top of his head and I open the door and I say *Why don't you come inside Joe?* It's friendly, I think, my tone. And he shakes his head."

"Do you remember did he look at you?"

"No I don't think he did. I'm pretty sure he was staring straight ahead. So I go back to doing whatever I'm doing and the storm gets worse until it's a blizzard and I go back and look out the window and there's Joe Sweeney still standing there. I think it's even dark by now, so I open the door and everything's just, you know how it is during a snowstorm, and Joe Sweeney is buried up to his knees in the snow and I say *You sure Joe you don't wanna come in*? And he just, same thing, shakes his head nope, and so at that point I give up and close the door. Oh and here's another strange thing."

"What's that?"

"He was wearing army fatigues. He had on green army fatigues with a, maybe a patch or something on the shoulder and the little, there was a little strip over the left pocket that said Sweeney."

"That's not so strange."

"You don't think?"

"No. I mean the guy *was* in the army."

"Was he? God, I guess you're right. He was."

"Just out of high school, I think. Before Vietnam was Vietnam."

"God, I had forgotten. There are so many things about him I've just . . . *forgotten*."

67

Dear Vim,

You're a hard guy to get a hold of these days so I thought I'd drop you a line to say hello and tell you some of the things I've been thinking about since I was out there in May. First I want to say how proud I am of you and how proud I was to be at your graduation. It meant a lot to be there and to see you take that Big Walk. You've grown into quite a guy (your mother will deny it but a lot of it must be those good Sweeney genes!).

Second I want to tell you I'm sorry. There is no other word for it, just sorry. I'm sorry because I know I was not there for you in a lot of ways growing up and I know I was not the best father. If I am being honest with myself—and I should also be honest with you—I must admit I was pretty bad at it actually.

But there are many ways in which a father can be "bad." My own father who of course died long before you were born was so cold and distant it was like living in the house with a stranger. I could not wait to leave home. And very early on I saw, shortly after you were born, some of his behaviors repeating themselves in me—or about to start repeating themselves—so I decided to leave before that could happen.

These are not excuses. I am only trying to be honest. I wanted to say some of this to you when I saw you but maybe it's easier to write it. We've never had a relationship but I want to have one. I know you don't know Meredith but she's a great person and she's been great for me, helping me realize many things. She's on your side. She misses you and would like to see more of you. We both would.

You are always welcome here. There is plenty of room for three.

Now that I've said this I hope you'll let me know what you think.

Also, I hope you'll excuse the following bit of "fatherly" advice (insert ominous music here), but your mother tells me you quit your job recently (and she is obviously the one who gave me your uncle's address) and that you have no plans to get another one. She told me she doesn't know if you're doing anything at all "productive" with your time up north.

Here goes:

Vim, I believe that by quitting your job you have wasted a good opportunity to get a head start on your future. College is hard and you have to be responsible. Not only in class but in how you pay for it. Meredith and I will try to contribute but at this point I don't know how much and I'm not sure you've demonstrated the right level of commitment. I'm sure your mother (and Ed) have already told you this.

The world does not meet people halfway.

A little bit of hard-earned wisdom (trust me!).

Again, it was great seeing you graduate. It always happens that too much time passes before we see each other—I know this has often been my fault but I am trying to be better in the future—so let's not have that happen again.

We miss you, Vim.

Love,
Dad

68

Down at the water's edge I got a line from the Pixies banging around in my head *in a place they say is dead in a lake that's like an ocean* I launch my voice at the water at the sky at the still-glowing moon and nothing changes. I shout my name into the wind as loud as I can and it flies right back at me and nothing changes. I send all my love and hatred, everything, all that I am, every second of my life, I scream it into the ether and it hangs there floating over the distant violet west then blows the fuck away like a cloud on a clear day and nothing really ever changes.

69

Time like wave after wave eroding us.

70

So we go to bed not knowing and wake up not knowing and from dream to dream everything goes wrong. Someone's sculpting my ice-block heart with a chainsaw.

71

Jake arrives at dusk under a sky like orange and blue sherbet but doesn't get out of the van. I watch through the window a while and he's only just sitting there. Finally I go out and get in the passenger seat. "Well?" he says.

"Pull on outta here and we'll just fucking go."

"Where to?"

"Eau Claire, Wisconsin."

"Never been there."

"Me either. It's just a place that exists in my mind."

"Actually, I think it's a real place."

"You know what I mean."

"What would you do in Eau Claire?"

"Maybe get another dishwashing job. Play music. Look at girls. Become the exact same person, in other words."

"I always forget how big Michigan is. It's so goddamn huge. You can drive north ten hours and still be in Michigan."

"Yeah but it's just trees up there. Trees and water. And militia dudes. You wanna go inside? You can meet Bro's girlfriend. We're gonna do build-your-own taco night." It's getting stuffy in the van so I roll down the window. "I guess we don't have to. We could sit in here the rest of the night."

Finally Jake turns to me and says: "What the fuck is wrong with you?"

"Exactly how do you mean that?" I say.

"I mean what the fuck are you doing at Wheeler's girl-friend's at seven in the morning screaming like a maniac and rolling around on the ground?"

I look away from him, toward the lake. "That seems like a thousand years ago."

"Yeah well. It wasn't. Fucking talk to me."

"I don't know what to say. I guess I fucked it."

"You *guess*? You *guess* you fucked it?"

"Yeah. What did they say?"

"Wheeler's, more than anything he's just totally confused. You know how he is, he's sweet that way. He went over about a thousand explanations and none of them seemed quite right. I said maybe you were on angel dust."

"I wasn't on angel dust."

"Scratch that one off the list then."

"What if I love her, Jake?"

"Who, Helene? Do you know that the parts of her body that aren't totally fucking scarred and self-mutilated have been sucked red by Wheeler's very own mouth?"

"Jake."

"Do you know that at least?"

"Yes, okay? I fucking, I know that."

"That chick is fucked," Jake says, "upstairs. And maybe that's Wheeler's thing but it ain't yours."

"Oh what's my thing then, Jake? Tell me."

"Maybe, I don't know, maybe trying to break up our band. Maybe that's your thing. Ever think of that? Ever think scream-ing at Wheeler and his girlfriend at seven in the morning might like, have bad repercussions?"

"Yeah. I thought of that. But only after the fact," I say. "I had my own shit going on upstairs. And I fucked it. I fucked it. But I didn't know how bad till afterward."

He takes a deep breath and doesn't say anything.

"So did you . . . drive all this way just to yell at me?"

"Yes. And also to build my own taco."

"What if I'm in love with her, Jake?"

He bursts into laughter. "Who the fuck do you think you're talking to?"

"My best friend," I say. "Now what if I'm in love with her?"

"I don't know, Vim. But let me ask you this question: What if you're not?"

A silence fills the van. "Let's go build tacos," I say, opening the door.

72

One margarita and it's like someone tucked my soul into nice clean flannel sheets. Two margaritas and my body expands, I become larger and a little warmer. Three and things are beautifully hazy and there is no more pain. After a fourth I want to take Cherie into the bedroom and eat guacamole off her ass crack.

Lick it, slam it, suck it.

73

On Mitchell St the sidewalk is wet from a brief rain and the pavement beneath the one stoplight dimly reflects red, yellow and green. Inside the Depot Tavern Jake and I stop at the bar while Bro and Cherie fall in with some friends in the back.

"First things fucking first." Jake, wearing mirrored aviator sunglasses, hands me a shot. "No i.d. I love this town. To rock," he says.

"And to roll."

And it burns going down.

With the peanut shells the floor resembles the surface of some weird planet. Over the bar is a mounted deer head, antlers draped with blinking blue Christmas lights.

"What's up with the glasses?" I say.

"It's a look."

"Lemme see."

"Hey not bad. Make a couple rounds with those on, you're golden."

"Yeah but I can't see shit."

"Sometimes you don't wanna see shit though, you know? Sometimes it's better to put up a few roadblocks and tell the world to fuck off."

A GUY WITH A COWBOY HAT and leather vest with nothing underneath and an apparently homemade tattoo of himself on

Grab On to Me Tightly as if I Knew the Way

his fleshy shoulder saying: "Shit I had a whore once stuck a beaded necklace up my ass said tell me mister when you're close so I fucked her like a piston like an iron fist till it was just about time and right then she grabs the last little bead on the end of the necklace and yanks that sumbitch like a lawn mower cord and holy damn shit I'm tellin ya buddy I sprayed her till her belly looked like modern art. I'm tellin ya I musta busted ten nuts at once."

"Don't you only have two though?" I say.

"You're quick buddy. You're quick."

"Where is the romance?" I say.

Laughter, choking, recovery.

"Where is the passion?"

"Romance, flowers, all that's for the bitches. But that's what they need. Women need a caring responsive compassionate person who appreciates their beauty. And not just the titties. Inner beauty too. And men. Men need a place to dump their glue."

Laughter, choking, recovery. He's wearing pointy cowboy boots with actual spurs that jingle as he crunches across the floor.

HAVING JUST PISSED and now feeling groovy I stand at the sink as hot water flows through my fingers. To the left of the mirror someone has written *Beatles vs Stones who wins?* So far it's eleven for the Beatles, seventeen for the Stones. I run wet hands through my hair and down the back of my neck. The door flies open and in walks a dude with super-gelled hair and a white polo shirt and he makes a huge production out of pulling out his dick, like it's so huge he's gotta do curls at the gym just for the strength to hold it to take a leak. He looks at me and says, "Nice shades."

"Thank you, baby."

"What was that?" he snaps, head whipping around, hair like a bed of nails.

"I meant baby as in homeboy."

He pisses for what must be a full minute and it's the same thing when he's done, shifting his whole body around to tame his cock and get it back down in his shorts.

"Somethin wrong with your hand? You cut yourself? Burn yourself? Man, one time I was at a party and this kid tried lightin a campfire with gasoline and long story short, that was the end of his face." He checks himself in the mirror, touches his dagger hair but of course it doesn't move. "Yeah, I seen some shit, all right. You can believe that. Anyway," nodding at the sink, "mind if I get in there?"

"I used all the soap."

"Didja now? Betcha also gotta flip a light switch on and off a thousand times before you can leave the room. OMD, right? I seen a guy like you on Sally Jesse or Montel or one of them shits, hell they're all the same ain't they."

"Beatles versus Stones who wins?"

"I tell ya, that's one contest I couldn't give a fuck about. I mean gimme some Bob Seger ya know? Yessir. Good old Uncle Bob."

"Tastes great or less filling?"

"Don't matter I'll drink whatever."

"Whopper or Big Mac?"

"I've always been more of a KFC man. Now lemme get a splash of that water. I don't need any goddamn soap." He wiggles his fingers under the tap and flicks water at the mirror, at our reflections. "Later days Willie Mays."

Grab On to Me Tightly as if I Knew the Way

"SO THE OLD BASTARD DROVE HIMSELF to the hospital he's having a heart attack at the kitchen table and I'm fucking flipped out and my mom and everyone and I'm like *Dad get in the car I'm driving* and he goes *No no you can ride shotgun just get me my keys.* So what could I do? I got him his keys. We're driving along and he's fucking around with the mirrors and the radio dial telling me to calm down because he's been through way worse shit and I'm like *Dad are you sure I think this is serious* and he cuts me off and gives me that shit-eating grin and sweat's just pouring out of him I mean his face is gray he looks half dead already and he says *Don't worry about me guy I'm gonna outlive every damn one of you.* And we roll into the driveway and pull up to the ER and he opens the door and falls right the fuck out of the car onto the pavement like a sack of potatoes."

"WHAT IS BEST IN LIFE?"

"To crush your enemies see them driven before you and to hear the lamentation of the women shit I fucked it ask me again."

"What is best in life?"

"To hear birds in the morning or you wake up and it's raining and the rain on the window going pitter-patter when it's cloudy and dark and your head's like a brick and you don't wanna move so you wait so you pull up the covers no this sounds way too gay I gotta start over I hate my voice ask me again."

"What is best in life?"

"To be at the movies at the East-Towne 5 and you're holding

her hand and you feel her blood going through her hand up into your body and the planets are crashing the world is dying but none of it matters the sound of her body it's humming the ions in the weird darkness her beauty could turn you to stone and you know without knowing that you are alive and what it means to be dead and you wanna go way out further than you've ever gone before but everything's gone or slipping away and holding on to love is like hugging fog I'm falling to pieces ask me again."

"What is best in life?"

"A bright white moon hovering over the swamp and the fireflies at the window all spelling your name and lighting the way to no fuck wait."

"What is best in life?"

"The longing the waiting the mystery the silence."

OVER AT THE BAR IS A PAIR of superfine knockers connected to a woman in a red V-neck shirt. Getting closer now I see freckles in the cleavage and it takes maybe five seconds to realize the woman is looking right at me and that her mouth is speaking words.

"Sorry, what?"

"I said why don'tcha take a picture it'll last longer."

And standing next to her, turning around now, is the guy from the bathroom, the meathead with hard hair and polo. He says, "Hey it's the hand-washer."

"Yeah, that's right." I'm smiling, holding a drink. "Cheers."

"What's the problem?" the guy says.

"I asked him why don't he take a picture."

"Picture of what?"

I say, "Well you know I don't really have my camera just now so."

"My boobs," she says.

He looks at her then looks at me. "What's this now?"

Again I smile, I shrug, as if to say: *Bitches, man.*

"Kid's *def*-initely a gawker," the woman says.

"Oh yeah. Well what's he gawkin at? What'cha gawkin at, gawker?" His arms are tanned cannons, his chest is a tank. "You checkin out my lady?"

"Lady? You his lady?" I say.

She rubs his big flexed muscle and says, "We're friendly."

"What the fuck," his voice rising, "I *said* are you checkin out my lady?"

I nod and flash the double thumbs-up. "Yes I am, homeboy. And she is *stacked*."

The woman's eyes narrow as if gazing out from the far shore of disgust. The dude's eyes on the other hand get very large and intense and he moves his head quickly back and forth like a pitcher shaking off signs. "What the fuck did you just say?"

Behind us someone says, "What did he just say?"

"Believe he said Lois is stacked."

Someone says, "Go easy, Spode. He's just a kid."

"Fuck you go easy," Spode replies. Then to me: "I asked you a question."

"Uh okay. Could you repeat the question, please?"

"Fuck you you fuckin smart-ass you heard me."

"Rod," Lois says, clutching his arm. "Come on."

"Yeah Spode, remember. I'm just a kid."

Spode's face is contorted and red. He moves away from the

bar. As if on cue, "When the Levee Breaks" comes on the juke-box. "Answer me Fuckhead!" he says.

"Answer you what?"

"What. The Fuck. Did you say. About my lady?"

"That's pretty good, Spode. But could you say it slower?"

"Ah shit," someone says.

"Kid you better fuckin shut it," says someone else.

Spode is very close now. A part of me's gotta be scared shitless but.

"Come on tough guy. Smart-ass. Tell me what you said."

Take a breath. Exhale. Remember what you wanted? Here come the fun times. "I *said,*" grabbing my dick and hefting it theatrically about, "five minutes with the king snake, Spode, and your lady sees god, motherfucker."

There isn't much room between me and the bar but he grabs me by the shirt and throws me against it and I must be as light as a toy and someone is saying *Taker easy Spode* and I wanna say sorry to the guy whose beer I just knocked over but Spode reaches back and I think someone grabs his arm the way his fist glances off me but he gets me again hard in the shoulder then connects with my face and the world jumps and crackles and goes out of focus and someone pulls me one way and another and another and I'm knocked to the floor where Spode tries to kick me but it's pretty much all over now but I can't say for sure because I'm blind from the tears and the pain and I can't hear anything over the huge crushing drums.

MY HEAD IN CHERIE'S LAP. She's pressing something cold and wet against my cheek. We're outside, on the sidewalk.

Mitchell St is silent and empty. The stoplight is blinking yellow. The sky is so low it seems like I could reach up and stab a finger through the fat gray clouds. I cough out words. "What happened in there?"

"I was about to ask you the same thing," Cherie says.

I blink. She disappears.

HER HANDS IN MY HAIR and touching my face. The whole left side of my body throbs and my head is sending out rays of pain from the center like one of those orbs in the Sharper Image catalog. A fine mist falls into my eyes.

"Hey there," Cherie says, "how do you feel?"

"Like an abortion," I say. And maybe then I black out again but I'm conscious enough to see certain faces coming from out of the darkness. I open my eyes.

"Penny Benjamin," I say.

"Who? No. This is Cherie."

"No I know," I say. "I know who it is."

A few minutes later I say, "Kim Deal."

"Who?" she says again.

"Helene Mollineaux."

"Is that that girl, your friend's girl?"

"And Anne Sweeney, my mother. Don't forget Anne Sweeney. And Trudy what the fuck. Wainwright. And Rachel from Charlevoix with a dog named Lucky who made me hide under her bed. And that chick in there with the, Lois, with the V-neck. The tits. And Nora Reperton. I'd . . . yeah. Nora Reperton. And now you. Cherie."

"Me?"

"What is your full name?"

"Cherie Bliss Bannister."

"And now you. Cherie Bliss Bannister."

"Okay I give up," she says. "Who are these people?"

"The women in my life."

THE WORDS REACH ME from somewhere. *Vim get up, Jake give me a hand here. Okay. One. Two. Three.* And then I'm on my feet, head rolling forward and then falling back, and it's full-on raining and I open my mouth and it rains down my throat. Cherie is here, bangs plastered in strands to her forehead. Jake is here. "How many fingers am I holding up?" he says. I look and see that it's only the middle one. "No more faggotry," he says.

"All right, what the fuck?" Bro says. "Can you stand?"

"A little bit. Why not?"

"Well I got good news and bad news," he says, rain dripping over his lips and down off his chin. He shakes his hair out and slicks it back. "The good news is that fucking Neanderthal Spode isn't gonna kill you. The bad news is, I am."

74

Whispers, cries, screams.

75

The first time I ever saw Bixby Wheeler we were all skating in the parking lot of the Gull Lake Church of Christ on the brand-new blacktop. He had dreadlocks then and I remember thinking: *A white dude with dreadlocks? No thanks.* But it was a hot day in the dead of summer and when he saw me glance at his Pepsi bottle, without a thought, without ever having met me, he held it out and asked if I wanted some. And we started talking and then we became friends. That was so long ago now, pre-everything.

76

So all right let's try it. There's no reason this moment can't matter. But every single one of them? Can't a guy just piss off the Bear River Bridge like Jake and I are doing now, our streams twinkling down into the abyss? There are too many fucking moments.

77

Driving alone in silence through the Upper Peninsula. I haven't seen a person or a car for the last hundred miles. It's a whole other world up here. Moose and black bear and beaver dams and men in camouflage stockpiling weapons for Armageddon. I've been alone for so long my thoughts are a wreck. But what can you do with all your bullshit hang-ups and hatreds in a landscape this beautiful?

78

Grand Marais is a one-road, no-stoplight town, right on Lake Superior. I first came here with Bro last summer when the Dream Police played a gig at the Dune Saloon. I pull off the main road and drive down a small hill to a small pond not far from the lake, a mini beachfront with a jungle gym and a swing set. The water's surface is glass-smooth. The houses on the other side of the pond look like Monopoly houses. The day, the air is so clear I see individual leaves on the trees. For a while, for a long time, I swing on the swing set, going higher and higher, finally launching myself out over the sand.

79

There is another kind of loneliness, the savage relentless kind. The kind that grabs you early and pulls you close in a cold embrace and never lets go. When I was younger and we still lived in Kalamazoo I'd walk across Inverness Lane to the playground and play in the sandbox for hours, just me, no brother, no sister, no neighborhood kids, just me surrounded by the rows of cream-colored buildings playing in the empty sandbox so utterly free and alone. I decided then I don't want anyone. The heart is paper and any jerk with half a face can call you a name and turn it to ashes.

80

Pictured Rocks National Lakeshore goes on for miles. The beach is made of rocks, not sand, and every rock looks like a tiny polished gem and there are signs up that say *Do Not Remove Under Penalty of Law*. This is why I drove the silent three and a half hours from Petoskey. I lie on my back on a bed of stones, arms out, legs crossed at the ankles, in the manner of dead JC. I scoop up big handfuls of rocks and let them drop and they fall through my fists and land like *click clatter click*.

Lake Superior and then beyond that is Canada. This is the end of MI, the end of the country, the end of the century. And the waves roll in like *shhh. Shhh. Shhh.* When I stand it's my first time ever on two feet. I fill my pockets with rocks till they're bulging, almost spilling out. This is why I came here and now I am going away.

81

A sign over the bar at the Dune Saloon says *Be Good or Be Gone*. The bartender's shirt says *If I Wanted to Listen to An Asshole I'd Fart*. The waitress is young, maybe my age, with black hair, perfect skin and a hideous car-sized hippie medallion hanging from a string on her neck. Between orders she stands at the bar and smokes and cracks wise with the old men on bar stools. There is a jukebox in the corner but no music. On my table are some rocks and a marble composition notebook purchased at a general store across the street. A hundred blank pages. I order food. I start writing.

82

Dearest most beautiful Baby,

Boot camp is hell—exile from the palace of your arms is worse than that—I wanna wake up next to you breathing your hair and skin, kissing your cheek and plus w/ my hand on your softly rising belly but no! I'm here instead running drills in the silver predawn misty swamps—just a boy in love and his M-16—only 6 more wks of this shit—bunking w/ Santiago and the rest of the goons and the DI calling me maggot and saying shit about my mom and latrine detail and babyshitbrown gravy at every sad meal—just 6 more wks and then who knows where they send me who knows where I end up but wherever it is every second away from you is a hammer punching my life—it's like gouging out my eyes—well they pretty much might as well if I can't look at you and I get so alone w/out you that life doesn't make one second of sense and I curse god and I curse time for always dragassing but I also know that only time can reunite us— once Uncle Sam is through w/ me and you're all done w/ beauty school—I know it won't be long really—I swear that when we come together our love will go out into space like a billion shimmering stars and no one will stop us ever.

Saving up a kiss
I am only yours,
v.

83

The waitress brings me a plate of steaming pasties, a northern MI delicacy, beef stew baked into a pie crust. "Whatcha writin?" she says.

"A letter," I tell her, closing the notebook.

"A letter? Who writes those anymore?"

"Nobody."

"You do."

"Yeah and I'm nobody."

"Nice to meetcha, Nobody. You want another Coke?" She reaches for my glass without waiting for a reply, taking a step toward the bar before pausing and looking back. "You know, you really aren't supposed to take those." She nods at the rocks. "It really is against the law and people get pissed, they write tickets. No joke. But don't worry. Your secret's safe with me."

84

Dear Mom,

I have traveled this far and have come to that part of life that recedes when you try to touch it. It's so huge and empty up here but the world is always looming, just beyond the

water's edge, just out of sight. And that's what I've been feel-
ing these last couple years, something big, bad and unknow-
able about to wash over me. And it's finally here. I just
shoved off in my pissant boat onto the huge rolling sea and
I'm letting my feet hang over and I'm dipping my toes and
it's

85

"Well someone was hungry," she says.

"Gotta get my fill now. No pasties in my neck of the woods."

"Where's your neck of the woods?"

"Down around Kalamazoo."

"Oh yeah, whattaya got down there?"

"Basically just a lotta Burger Kings."

"I like Burger King."

"Me too."

"You're a ways from home. What brings ya to Grand Marais?"

"Nothing really, just seeing the sights."

"Everyone comes for the Pictured Rocks."

"Why do you say it like that?"

"Like what?"

"Like you think it's so boring."

"I grew up here. I got a right to be bored if I want."

"Yeah but it's so, you look out and it's just so. Wow."

"It's looked like that my whole life."

"I've never seen so much empty space."

"How much empty space ya wanna see?"

"You're in the middle of nowhere."

"Yeah I am. And right there's the problem."

"Doesn't seem like such a problem to me."

"All I can say is try living here."

"Maybe I will someday."

"Your name's not really Nobody."

"No."

"So what is it?"

"Simon Ritchie. What's yours?"

"Abigail."

"Abigail. That's a nice name."

"No it's not. I hate it."

"Don't."

"Why?"

"Because it's beautiful."

"Ya think?"

"Yeah I think."

"How long ya in town for, Simon?"

"About ten more minutes."

86

Dear Dad
  Dad
  Dear Joe
  JS
  Father
  Dear Father
  Dear Dad
  Dad,
  All this time all these years and so much anger . . .

87

I tear the first page out of the notebook and put it in an envelope, already addressed, stamped and ready to go. 33 Mangrove Way. Before sealing I drop in four of the tiniest prettiest rocks. This is my heart, my apology. I push back from the table after throwing down bills for the meal, leaving a fifty percent tip. Abigail is standing at the end of the bar and I walk over and hand her a note and she looks at me smiling and says, "What's this?"

"Open it after I'm gone," I say.

"Are you leaving now?" she says.

"Yeah."

"Goin back to Kalamazoo?"

"No, not just yet."

"It's weird, Simon, I don't know you at all, you're a total stranger but."

"But what?"

"Nothing," she says.

"Don't hate your name," I tell her again.

She doesn't say anything. She looks at the note.

"Why don't we . . . shake hands," I say.

"Okay." We shake hands, holding on a little longer than necessary.

"See ya round, Simon," Abigail says.

"No you won't," I say.

"Yeah but maybe someday though," she says.

88

Abigail,
    The world is a far greater place than I ever imagined.
And it is yours.

89

Bro's hand on Cherie's knee. He leans close and whispers something that makes her smile. She whispers back. He takes *Are You Experienced* from its worn sleeve but only plays one song and it fills the room, this song, with a desperate inconceivable beauty. I see sadness everywhere, even in my own empty hands. Through the open window I see moonlight, starlight, a car with one headlight. Everyone I know is made of light.

90

I'm up so early it's still dark and down at Dawn Donuts it's still Althea's shift, except now she has a helper and the counter is packed. Nelson Maddox is there.

"Hey Darby! What's up, my man?"

The radio is on and there is so much noise. Cheap Trick doing Elvis, the voices, the pinball machine, I love it. I thought I wanted silence but now, no. I thought I wanted to play alone in the sandbox forever. Give me a map back to civilization and a package of jerky. Set me on fire and I'll light my own way.

"Nelson, do you ever sleep?" I say.

"Oh yeah. Sometimes. Sometimes I get an hour or two here and there." He shrugs, looking genuinely sad. "It's a hard thing. But you're kind of a vampire too. What brings you out at this hour? Here, man, let's take a seat."

I get a coffee and we move to one of the booths. Nelson says, "What the fuck happened to your face?"

"I had a run-in at the Depot Tavern."

"No shit?"

"Yeah. I was . . . running off at the mouth to a big guy named Spode."

"Rod Spode? I know that son of a bitch. He sells like, luxury boats to the Fudgie crowd. Always seemed like an okay guy to me. Bit of a meathead but generally okay."

"Could be. I was at fault."

"Too many beers?" says Nelson.

"Something like that."

"Well good, man. Good for you. It takes a big man to admit he's in the wrong. But let this be a lesson. Bad things happen when you leave Dawn Donuts." He laughs and runs his hands over the table. "This place is like a, what do you call it. Sanctuary."

I pause, sipping my coffee. It tastes perfect.

"Nelson, I'm gonna tell you something now."

"Okie-doke," he says. "Shoot."

"It's a secret," I say.

For a moment he only looks at me. He leans back and puts his arms up on the booth behind him and his knees knock into mine as he stretches out. "Whup, sorry," he says, shifting slightly. Now he's ready to listen. His face has changed, eyes like I haven't seen them before these few times we've talked, saying *Take whatever you don't want and throw it away, throw it into me, let me have it, fill me with all that you want to let go of.*

"It starts with . . . it starts with my name," I say.

91

The razor-thin line between the last gasp of night and sunrise. The sun breaking over a field on your left, bleeding light back into the dead world. The pale moon still hanging. The way the lake and the sky are at this second identically blue.

The motor hums, drowning language.

The Flapjack Shack. The Griddle Haus. The River Bottom Roadside Restaurant.

The deep hunger you feel that touches every nerve, every cell, a hunger that can't be sated. The way you feel this hunger always, even in sleep.

The antique stand. The U-pick raspberry stand. The wind. The wind smells of water and pine. The green leaves licking white clouds. The gas station with one pump and no attendant and a self-service sign. The radio static. The wind.

The sense of oneness and wonder and contentment.

The way it never lasts.

The way the future can't be lived, it only hovers before you, everywhere around you, like a note of music, a guitar chord struck, a thing that can't be seen or touched.

The smell of bacon and coffee as you enter the Real

McCoy. The ten-egg omelet. The full pot of coffee the waitress leaves at your table. The waitress Evelyn as object of sexual desire. The monstrous, exhausting, life-affirming dump you take in the Real McCoy bathroom. The toilet so high it feels like a throne.

The joy you feel as you leave the restaurant and the sun hits your face and you get back in the Subaru and back on the road.

The way you fly down 131, winding once again through Grand Rapids and then back out of it. The familiar landscape somehow transformed.

The bright potted flowers along the sidewalks of Plainwell.

The deep green valleys on either side of M-89.

The fatigue setting in, the emptiness, the dull panic, an alarm clock blaring, banging against the love and desire. The certain knowledge that all of these things will live within you and fight for dominance the rest of your days.

The throbbing in your face and shoulder. The wind. The fatigue. The once-yellow fence around the driveway of your house. The way you left little crumbs of yourself in your wake to remember the way to get back.

92

"So did you find what you were looking for?" she says.

"I don't know. That all depends."

"On what?"

"I guess on what I was looking for."

"Are you saying you don't know what that is?"

"No. I'm just saying . . . I'm saying why does it always have to be like that?"

"Like what?"

"Like why do I have to always be *looking* for something?"

"Well," my mother says, "aren't you?"

93

Downtown Kalamazoo painted on a wall on the side of a store called the New York Collection a chorus line of dancing cartoon apple-men with toothy smiles and top hats and canes and beaming from the eyes of the apple-man on the far left for as long as I can remember are the spray-painted words *Riot Now*.

94

New set of 10-gauge Boomers, two for the price of one at Moreno's. Two new nine-volt batteries, one for the tuner, one for the Rat. A dozen new Tortex picks, yellow, with the feeling of brand-new picks, stiff and a little powdery.

95

Mr Wheeler steps out onto the front porch in shorts and sandals with black socks pulled up to the calves of his white, hairless legs. He squints, shielding his eyes from the sun's glare, and tells me that Bixby is still asleep. I glance at my wrist.

"Two o'clock," he says, noticing I don't have a watch.

"Is he . . . alone?" I say.

Mr Wheeler shrugs. "To tell you the truth, Vim, I really don't know what he is. But you can go on in and find out."

I walk through the living room and down the narrow hallway. On Wheeler's door are an ad for the Jesus Lizard "Wheelchair Epidemic" seven-inch and the picture of him in a dress from the *Gazette* and little stickers of the old Mr T cartoon. Mr T and his squad of crime-fighting gymnasts. I drum my fingers on the door and wait. A stirring, a groan, a mattress squeak. I knock again and Wheeler, barely audible, goes: "Yeah?"

In my best Mr Wheeler impression, superflat and nasally, I say, "Bixby, wake up. It's Christmas morning. Come and see what Santa brought you."

"Gimme a break, dad."

"Wheeler, I'm kidding. It's me."

"Vim?"

"Yeah."

"Go away, man. I'm sleeping."

"Not anymore, you're not."

"I'm tired. I was up till five."

"You know, you can't make up sleep. You either get it or you don't."

"That's the point, man. I'm *getting* it."

"Let me in."

At last he opens the door. The air in the room is heavy and close and reeks of the musty essence of a thousand Wheelers. The hazy blind-fractured light spilling in across the walls and floor reminds me of the scene in *Apocalypse Now* where Martin Sheen does drunken karate and breaks the mirror with his fist. Wheeler's in his boxers, scanning the floor for something to wear. "We have to quit meeting like this," he says.

Helene's hickeys or love marks or whatever he calls them are still visible, about a dozen fading strawberry birthmarks. Wheeler digs out his old Joy Division *Unknown Pleasures* T-shirt and slips it on. He pushes the sheets and blankets into a pile in the corner of the bed and sinks into it. I sit backward in the room's one chair.

"So how you doing?" he says.

"Okay. I just got back. I went up north for a while."

"I heard. How was it?"

"It was uh . . . restorative. In some ways."

"Well that sounds good. Looks like someone might've popped you one."

"That was the non-restorative part. Do you mind if I open a window?"

"No, go ahead. I had them open earlier but my dad was doing all his lawn shit. It was so fucking loud it was like he was *in* my room with his weedwhacker."

"There we go. That's better."

"It was like he was holding the weedwhacker up to my screen just to spite me."

"Out on the porch just now he told me he doesn't know what you are."

Wheeler's face clouds over. "He said that?"

"No," I say. "He didn't. It was just . . . it was a dumb joke."

"Ah yeah. Vim Sweeney and all the kidding. So was that whole scene over at Helene's, was that like, another one of your hilarious jokes?"

"Yeah," I say, clearing my throat, "about that."

"Yeah?"

"I'm really . . . shit. I would like to tell you I'm sorry."

"You would like to or is that what you're actually telling me?"

"No. That's what I'm actually telling you. I am here now to say that I'm sorry. Wheeler. Fuck. This has been," I pause and take a deep breath and think about exactly what I want to say. Only now do I realize I want to tell Wheeler the truth, in a way. Not the whole truth but a version of it. "The last couple months have been a . . . strange time for me and I, for some reason I gravitated toward Helene, not necessarily out of some romantic or sexual thing but because she had a presence—she *has* a presence—and I thought, I mean I perceived on some level that she and I could . . . relate somehow and . . . you know the rest."

"No I don't, Vim. Why don't you tell me." His tone is neutral. I search for clues as to what he might be thinking but Wheeler only stares at me, unblinking.

"Okay," I say, licking my dry lips, "I mean as long as you're making me say it, the next thing is me showing up at Helene's and freaking the fuck out after staying up all night and drinking enough caffeine to cause a heart attack and driving back and forth on I-94 like it was a go-cart track. Like I was fucking insane."

A strange, prickly feeling overwhelms me as the words flow, like spiders crawling around in my bones. A long silence follows.

"So it's not some sexual thing," Wheeler says. "So tell me. What would have happened if I hadn't been there? What is it you wanted from her, Vim?" He looks at me until I look away. "Or what do you want from her still?"

"Someone to listen, Wheeler. That's all. Just someone to listen."

"So call a fucking hotline," he says.

"I wanted someone to . . . understand."

"Understand what? You? How deep you are?"

"Wheeler, no. Listen. There are things happening inside my brain that you don't, that you couldn't possibly understand. And I'm not trying to be arrogant here, I'm just saying how could *you* possibly understand when *I* don't fucking understand? I don't understand myself. Okay? I don't know what I want. I don't know why I'm here."

"You mean here in my room?" he says. "Because I can answer that one easy."

"No, asshole. I mean *Here*."

Wheeler clasps his hands behind his head and stares at the ceiling. "All right. Now it's your turn to listen. One day I woke up and my mom told me she was going away for a while, on a trip to New Mexico. She told me she just had to get away. It's not your fault, she said, it's not anybody's fault. She was just feeling a little burned out. All right, yeah, mom, sure. I'll see you when you get back. That was four years ago. So now it's just me and my old man. And me and my old man, we don't even talk now. Unless we have to. Are you hungry? Yes. Turn your music down. Fine."

As Wheeler is talking it occurs to me that Jake's parents may be the only ones I know who are still together and doing okay. How can so many people fall out of love?

"And then, you know, time passes. And one day I wake up and realize I don't wanna hang around with a bunch of fake-shit Christian hypocrites anymore. And be taught by a bunch of god-squadders who only like kids who play soccer and call me, you know, pretty much call me a fucking faggot behind my back. So I quit. I dropped out. It was the scariest thing I ever did in my life. Some people think it's stupid or cowardly or lazy or whatever but. It's scary. And now I gotta like, live with my decision. The same way I gotta live with dear old dad for two more years, till I can move out and . . . I don't know what. Do my own thing."

He sits up and wipes at the tears spilling down his cheeks. I'm surprised to see him crying. His voice is very much under control.

"So don't come into my room and tell me what a strange time in your life it is or how there's things I don't understand. I'm sure there's plenty of shit about you I don't understand. But you know what? I don't give a fuck. My own life is strange enough. And right now I'm just trying to fight my way through it. And as far as why you're here."

A whiny, high-pitched buzz. His dad is in the yard, working some machine.

"Fuck!" Wheeler says. *"Do you see?"*

He slams down the window and flips off his dad through the wall. *"Fuck!"* he says again, tugging at little bits of his hair. Finally he sighs; he laughs darkly.

"I don't know why you're here, Vim. I don't know why anybody's here. I just know that in this world. Man, this world is so fucked that you just . . . gotta be good to people. And then good stuff . . . the hope is that good things come your way."

"Like a karma kinda thing?" I say.

"Yeah. I guess so."

"Wheeler," I say, staring at the floor. "Wheeler, I'm truly sorry. I am."

There is another long silence. The sun continues to beat through the blinds and with the windows closed the room heats up again. Now, in addition to Wheeler-musk, it smells like gasoline and whacked weeds and dirt. Wheeler is the first to speak.

"Do you wanna play music?" he says.

I glance around the room. "Now?"

"Yeah. Why? Where else you gotta be?"

"Nowhere." I shake my head, grinning. "Absolutely fucking nowhere."

So we go to the basement and bash it out. Ordinarily I don't jam but it can be great what happens when you shut off your brain and let the music come. An hour or so later we have a new song and it's a huge leap forward, a breakthrough of sorts. I hum the lyrics to myself as we play it over and over again.

> *I had a good life*
> *I had a good life*
> *I had a good life but I was underfed*

I had a
Would you excuse me? Do you believe me?
Life is a movie and dying is TV.

96

Another five-page spread about this motherfucker? With all-new testimonials and full-color photos? Did I fall asleep for a hundred years and he cured AIDS or something? Or is he still just basically throwing a ball around a field, playing a child's game?

97

Tonight is vast and warm and meaningless. My mom snaps through another days-old newspaper. I'm dozing in the recliner, watching Ed in the kitchen making peanut butter and butter sandwiches for his lunch tomorrow. He licks the excess peanut butter off the knife before washing it. He blows the plastic baggies open and puts the sandwiches into the baggies and then into his blue Igloo lunch cooler. I wish I could make my hands a snow globe and hold this moment under glass forever.

98

I awaken in the dark with hands on my head, fingers in my hair, and my heart grabs. The windows and blinds are open. A broad patch of moonlight falls across the bed. I sit up quickly, terrified, disoriented, and a gentle hand on my back stops me as surely as if it were a knife. The hand moves up to my neck, over my shoulders, then back down. I know who it is then. I turn toward her. "*Surprise,*" Helene whispers.

She touches my face with the backs of her fingers. I open my mouth but say nothing. Sleep falls away. A minute passes, two, three. I lie back on the bed and breathe in deeply the smell of the mist and the night and her hair and her skin. Her body is warm. Her weight is pressed against me.

"How did you get in?" I say.

"I found the spare key."

"What? That's impossible."

"Is it?"

"Yes."

"Okay. But here I am."

"I've gotta be dreaming. This can't be happening."

"You are not dreaming," she says.

"You can't have found that key."

"The one behind the light switch in the garage, that key?"

"That's fucking impossible," I say.

"Is it?" She holds the key up and the dangling Pearl Paper keychain it's attached to glints in the moonlight.

"I must've told you. I can't . . . remember now but I must have."

"You didn't."

"How'd you get in here and my parents didn't hear you?"

"I got to the hallway and stopped between the two rooms. One door was open and the other one closed. Your dad's quite a snorer."

"Stepdad," I say.

"Stepdad."

"You are blowing my fucking mind into pieces."

"I stood in the hallway for a long time, holding my breath. Your parents didn't move. I thought *Vim's the kinda guy who sleeps with his door closed.* So I put my ear to the door. All I could hear was the fan. Finally I came into the room. At first I stood in the corner and just watched and you were so still and quiet it was like you were dead. I wanted to shake you, not violently or anything, just a little shake, a touch, like when your mom used to get you up in the morning for school."

"Were you in my room then too?"

"No. I'm only here now."

"I don't ever want you to leave."

"I'm going to have to," she says. "Eventually. But I'm here right now."

My mind is shattered. I shut my eyes tightly and open them and watch the dim shapes falling like slow-motion rain till they stop a second later and I look at her again. "You must be a dream," I say. "I was dreaming you and then you appeared."

"Touch me, Vim," she whispers. "See if I'm a dream."

•   •   •

SHE MOVES HER HAND SLOWLY over my chest and arms. I stroke her hair, tuck a strand behind her ear, straighten it, tuck it back behind her ear. She blinks against my ribs, butterfly kisses. I put the tip of her pinky to my lips and kiss. She opens my hand, whispers into the palm, and I feel the words she's saying, the heat of her breath, but can't hear what they are. I breathe in deeply. She presses against me, holding tightly with both arms. I lie on my stomach and she lies on my back, her lips against my face. I hide in her hair. She tucks her hands down under my shoulders. Whenever she moves I feel her breasts and hips and knees and toes. I feel the weight of who she is, all that she's known and done and lived on earth. She kisses my shoulder, a phantom kiss, barely touching the skin. The whole time we hear Ed snoring through the wall.

"Why are you here?" I say.

"Because," she says, "I wanted to see. I wanted to lay with you."

"It's *lie*."

She pauses. "I'm not lying."

"No. I mean it's *lie*. You wanted to *lie* with me."

"Shut up," she tells me.

"VIM?"

"Yeah?"

"Come back to me."

"I'm here."

"You were sleeping."

"I wasn't."

"You were."

"I was resting my eyes."

"We don't have much time."

"Yeah we do. Sure we do. We have all the time in the world."

"We don't. I have to go pretty soon."

"You don't. We can rest for a while, then get up and have a leisurely breakfast."

"Who, me and your parents?"

"Yeah. Or if you want I can take off and it can just be the three of you."

"You feel good. Your body is so warm."

"Your body feels better," I say.

"And you're sweet too. I never thought you'd be this sweet."

"So you thought about me?"

"Nope. Not once. I never thought about you."

"What about Wheeler?" I say.

"No," shaking her head, pressing a finger to my lips, "don't say that name. I only want you to hold me," Helene says.

I tell her I am, I am holding her.

"No hold me more hold me tighter."

"Why did you come here?" I say.

"Because," she says, "I wanted to *lie* with you."

"You have to tell me. You're not being fair. Please tell me why."

"You came to me first don't forget you started it all hold me tighter."

"Please," I say, holding her tightly, so tightly I'm afraid she'll break, and she's trying to smother me too, her arms pulling me in when I can't get any closer and the sheet is tangled around our ankles, tying our feet together too.

Grab On to Me Tightly as if I Knew the Way

"I wanted to be the first one to say it even before your mom or anyone I wanted you to hear it from my mouth first."

"Hear what?"

"Happy Birthday," she says.

She kisses my cheek and rolls over and over.

99

Shortly after we're seated at the Olive Garden my mom leaves the table and returns a moment later looking super relaxed and nonchalant. She opens the menu and starts scanning it like it's the most interesting thing she's ever seen.

"What'd you just do?" I say.

"Me? Nothing. I went to the bathroom. You guys know what you want?"

"Did you go tell the people to come out and sing 'Happy Birthday'?"

"No. Of course not," she scoffs.

We've been through this before. In fact it happened just last year. And the year before that and the year before that etc., only those times were at Chi-Chi's, which was my birthday spot till they brought in this OG and set it right down in the heart of the awful sprawl in Portage. Maybe next year I'll shoot for Bennigan's.

"Mom?" I say.

"Yes?" she says, mimicking my tone.

"This is your only son, here. Your only child. Now look me in the eyes and tell me the truth."

"I *am* telling the truth."

"Did you go tell the people?"

"Vim, don't be silly."

"Because you know I hate that. You do it every year and I hate it."

"I *know*. You already told me in the car ten times."

Ed unfolds his napkin and spreads it in his lap, though there's nothing on the table, not even water glasses. "If I was you, partner, I'd get ready for some singin."

I glance around the restaurant suspiciously. Every person I see looks in on the cabal, like they're ready to spit their food onto their plates and break into song. Here comes the waitress. Look at that shiny alien made-up smile. I'm so fucking dead. She takes our drink orders and brings the basket of breadsticks and the bottomless salad bowl. The plate-sized pin on her shirt says *Hospitaliano!*

I remember reading somewhere that that isn't even a word.

A minute later I'm totally full and almost can't eat another bite. But the shit keeps coming. I eat many other bites. So many fucking breadsticks. No one can stop. They're like salted crack logs. I'm double-fisting, one in each hand, going into either side of my mouth. Ed dips breadsticks in his beer. My mom tears them into pieces and eats the pieces off her plate. The second we finish a basket, another one appears. This happens ten times. We're averaging a basket of breadsticks per minute. They must have a whole breadstick wing here, a whole fleet of people whose job is only to crank out breadsticks. *Oh and what do you do?*

I'm a breadstick technician out at the OG on Westnedge.

I tear one in half and sop up the dressing at the bottom of our bottomless salad bowl. My mom flags down the waitress. More salad, please. I can't believe how much I've eaten. Yet here is a third Pepsi, another bowl of salad, our Taste of Tuscany sampler platter, my veal parmesan, more breadsticks. Hey there. I open the maroon napkin and eat three more. Ed sits back halfway through his lasagna, tiny drops of sweat breaking out on his forehead. He sighs deeply, looking pained.

"How do you feel?" my mom asks him.

"Like I'd like to puke," he says.

But he orders another beer. My mom orders more wine. And how about me, would I maybe care for another Pepsi? Why the fuck not, honey? Hospitaliano!

When the orgy of eating is over the waitress and a busboy clear our plates.

"What about dessert?" I say.

My mom waves it off. "Not for me. I'm stuffed."

"Maybe I'll get a coffee," Ed says. He looks at the waitress. "I'll have a coffee."

"And I'll have the tiramisu," I say.

"No," says my mother.

"No?"

"No. We have a nice cake at home."

"We do? Since when?"

The waitress and my mom exchange quick, grave glances and then the waitress retreats. I know what's coming and already I'm blushing and a little bit pissed but it's too late to protest. A group of way too happy OG wage-slavers suddenly appears and falls in around me, seems like thirty of these motherfuckers, belting out the words to some birthday song that isn't "Happy Birthday." Someone puts a cake in front of me with a single candle in it. My mom and Ed are grinning and there's a glint in Ed's eye like *I know, pal, I'm with you, but you just gotta get through the next twenty seconds.* And I do. The people stop singing and start clapping and everyone else in the room, all the other diners, follows suit. "Make a wish," the waitress says.

The word flies through me and burns the nerve centers, like the flame of this little candle. I was born and I've lived eighteen years. But it's not an Alice Cooper song. It's my life. Sorry, Bro. And you know what else? You can wish in one hand and shit in the other. And I'm smiling now. I'm filled with love. I blow out the candle and the waitress cuts the cake.

100

The phone rings and I hear your voice. Yeah I know you. I'm even like you, I'm told. My mother says this from time to time, usually in like a negative or tired or sadly ironic kind of way. God, she'll say, you can be just like Joe Sweeney. Which I always think is weird, on account of the obvious, don't you? So the bad shit's written on the DNA.

"Hey there," you say when I answer the phone.

"Hi," I say.

I knew the call was coming, had been expecting it, and as soon as the phone rang I knew, crashed out on the living room floor, still stuffed with OG, gazing at the ceiling with a feeling of pleasant dislocation, I knew.

Let me tell you how I feel when I hear your voice. And this is going way back to a time before I knew how I felt about any of this. If I even know now.

I feel *dread*. I feel *confusion*. I feel *guilt*. I feel *sadness*. I feel the systems begin to churn and move forward at high speeds beyond my control, as if my stomach were a compass in a room with a giant magnet, as if . . .

"How you doing?" you say.

"Happy Birthday!" you say.

"Thank you," I say.

"This is the big one. This is a milestone. This is, so what, now I guess you can buy dirty magazines and go fight in wars. Oh and vote! Don't forget that one. I mean come on, let's, we gotta prioritize here. Lucky for you there's an election coming up."

"Yeah," I say, forcing a little laugh, "what luck."

"Forget dirty magazines. Bill Clinton or George Bush? There's the real fun."

And now it's your turn to laugh, a low dry chuckle.

"Yeah. I mean wow. Think of everything I have to look forward to."

"Better start reading up now so you can make an informed choice," you say. And you laugh again and I laugh again and when the laughter fades you say, "No but seriously, Vim. How are you? How have you been?"

But seriously, folks . . . what's up with airplane food?

"I've been good. Things have been, you know, pretty much the same. I went up north for a while, visited my uncle, came back. Now I'm just uh."

"How's your uncle doing?"

"Oh. He's . . ."

We talk for a minute or two about my uncle and his crazy ways and the few things you remember from your time in the family, how the first time you met my uncle and his brother you thought, I mean these guys were gone, Vim, they looked like they were about to pass out at the table. I'd tried pot just a time or two but nothing like what these guys or kids, I should say, I guess really they were just kids at the time and . . .

I'm nodding, smiling, thinking of the spaghetti. My mom walks into the kitchen and as she passes she looks and whispers: *"Joe Sweeney?"* Then she's at the sink, rinsing her coffee cup and couldn't care less. She's already been through it. I'm on my own.

You are my family. Your name is in mine. Your blood is in mine. The telephone turns into a hammer. "What'd you do today," you say, "anything special?"

"Special?" I say.

"Yeah you know, did you go out to eat or anything or . . ."

"We went out."

"Oh yeah? Where'd you go?"

"The Olive Garden."

And this for some reason makes you laugh. You *laugh.* Maybe I can't read the laugh. Maybe it's nothing. Or maybe you're laughing because it's all we know how to do. But the laugh cuts me deep, my thoughts jumble and swarm, the kitchen reels.

"Pretty fancy," you say, still amused.

"Fancy?" I look around the room. Nothing in here makes sense anymore. The phone isn't a hammer, it's a giant sucking heart.

"All-you-can-eat breadsticks," you say. "Can't beat that."

I think of my mom. I think of Ed Hoekstra. I think of a time not so long ago, early last fall. I was on the back porch and Ed came home from some golf thing. He can't golf. I'm a hacker, he likes to say, but I drink beer pretty good. And he was drunk then so we shot the shit for a while and his eyes were swimmy and happy before they changed and he looked over at me and said in a low voice *You know it Vim, you know it, don't you?*

I didn't speak. I waited for him to finish. But he did not finish. During the pause my mind rolled back in fast-breaking waves the way it's doing right now and Ed wiped his face where a tear had fallen. I felt very small, like I didn't know shit, and I waited.

You know I love you just like . . . like you were my own son.

So now a huge hole opens and the truth flies up from my throat and bangs against the back of my teeth and all the rage and denial. Sometimes I think there's no place for truth in the world, no place for love. But I want you to know me finally in a way you never have, because some wounds don't heal and some dreams won't die and I want you to know me. I want you to understand or try to as much as you can so we can go on reflecting one another but in different places, a different geography separated forever by unbridgeable distances so I say to you now, "Yeah, no, you sure can't. But tell me, how would you like all you can eat of my dick?"

And the next thing is I'm shaking in some other room and my mother comes over and then she has her arms around me.

101

The next day there is a card in the mailbox. Inside the card is a check from the account of Joseph A. Sweeney and Meredith M. Haverchuck written in the amount of $500. The memo on the check says *Welcome to the Club!* and the note in the card says

> *Vim,*
>   *Here's a little something to get you started on the road to adulthood (uh-oh!).*
>   *Happy Birthday!*
>
>   *Love,*
>   *Dad*

Then, in loopy, smeared script, as if written left-handed:

> *Would love to see you soon! Have a special day! Enjoy it!*
>   *Meredith*

102

All the young punks out on the sidewalk, roaming in hordes over from Bronson Park, crossing Michigan Avenue in heavy traffic, skating, smoking, swearing, tattooed. Ain't that America. Bimbo's Pizza is next door to Club Soda, so close they share a T-shaped front entrance. Framed photos of old Kalamazoo on the walls, early Beatles or other oldies always on the jukebox. Plus they have a bathroom with a locking door and a plug-in air freshener and soap always in the dispenser. A must.

This is our first Monday New Music Night. Vine is the headliner and we're next to last. The opening band, Urination of Sharon, has already started. I've always hated the UOS singer, a slumming ex-mall dude who yelps lyrics about sexism on television in a voice like a dachshund getting raped up the butt with no lube.

Ellroy Marx blows into Bimbo's and takes in the scene, looking malnourished and exhausted, yet somehow still above the fray. He's got his Public Enemy hat and a Laughing Hyenas T-shirt, lording over his kingdom.

"This is war, dude. Okay? I'm talking, this is the cooption of a whole, of our whole culture and for what? So fuckin Kurt Cobain can see himself on MTV?"

"Yeah but it's, I mean, is it really Kurt's fault, I mean it's art."

"Dude. Listen to me."

"I mean he just, he wrote some songs, didn't he, isn't that all he."

"It ain't art if you can buy it at Kmart."

Helene is wearing oversized sunglasses and a red feather boa. She pours half-and-half into her coffee, then stirs it and sticks the wet spoon upside down in her mouth.

Wheeler flips through an old issue of *MRR,* barely glancing at the pages. The whole table is trembling slightly from the constant insane bouncing of his leg. Every minute or two he looks up, looks around, takes a big deep breath.

Jake eyes a fresh new crop of emo chicks, all with black Xs on their hands, bleached hair, big jeans and tight T-shirts. "Give em another year or two," he says.

Helene glances over. "What do you mean?"

"These straight-edge chicks, man. No drugs or drink? It's untenable. I've seen it before. They go to one party, try a cigarette, sip a beer. Pretty soon they're fucking chain-smoking and dropping acid and sucking malt liquor down like it's mother's milk."

"What about the dudes?"

"They tend to stick with it. Some of them anyway. The real true pussies."

"So it's only the girls who have no resolve?"

"To what? Not have fun? No, I'm just saying the girls fall harder."

"When they fall at all," Helene says.

Arthur Motts, the Vine singer, walks in, followed by a young beret-sporting acolyte. Motts is talking about something Russian and how there's a poet he loves who shot himself in the heart, as usual tossing out words like *postmodern* and *futurism.*

Wheeler starts tearing pages out of the *MRR.* "Fuck it," he says.

"Fuck what?" I say.

No answer.

Helene's hand shakes as she raises the coffee cup to her lips, eyes hidden behind the big black lenses. There is an element of late modern Bono in her look that I'm sure she'd be pissed if I mentioned. She's got her fingers in the boa. She brushes it lightly against her nose, saying, "How could I have ever lived without one of these?"

"What a terrific question," I say. "Life without a feather boa sure doesn't sound like life to me. In other news, half the world is starving."

"There's that rapier wit again." She makes a gun with her finger and thumb and aims it right at me. "Bang," she says.

Wheeler watches this. He leans over and touches her arm, rubs her leg under the table, which for the moment has stopped shaking. They stare into each other and smile. I see them as if from the bottom of the ocean, thinking about the predawn hours of my birthday, wondering what happened to that feeling, the sense that Helene and I were alive for a reason, made to kiss and love and be together.

Why do I cling hopelessly to this ghost?

"Because it's so much more than *music*. So much more than just *entertainment*. Okay? This is our identity. Our lifeblood and what, we're supposed to just fucking sit here and let MTV and fucking *Rolling Stone* and some fucking A&R guy with a coke spoon up his ass and a gold ring on every finger take this all away from us?"

"No but I mean if you look at it a different way, from just a bit of a slightly different perspective, you know, it's like Kurt is just."

"Because I'm sorry okay excuse me but that is *bullshit*."

"I mean he's just a guy like us who wrote some songs."

"A guy like *us*? Are you *insane*?"

"Well no but."

"Hold on a second here. Remind me again how much you're making at Bunca Car Wash, if you could just for a second refresh my memory."

"It's not a ton, you know, it's not, obviously I'm not making Kurt money but."

"Oh that's right. You're making *minimum fucking wage*."

The door opens. A quick blast of UOS, one of two songs in their repertoire written from the point of view of a slave. "Plantation," it's called. No one is talking. Wheeler stops tearing and puts his hands on the table, which is bouncing again. The jukebox clicks over. "Norwegian Wood." Never have I felt more divided, more like I was drowning, yet at the same time breathing in great golden light. Beauty exists, so does pain. And you can live through both and feel the same sting and wonder.

Helene sighs, sips coffee, chews her lip.

When they fall at all.

THE MIC TASTES LIKE beer and smoke. "Check one two check check." We're tuned, ready. Jake does a few bars of "Ceremony." At the edge of the stage there's a row of blinding white band T-shirts, five or so, lined up like punk rock billboards. Beyond that a hazy darkness. But I know you're out there, claws out, you and your slavering army.

I'm no longer thinking. I'm dreaming the noise.

We've never played through a sound system this good. Jake

leaps onto a monitor and flies back and the stage shakes when he lands. Wheeler's never attacked his kit with this ferocity. At one point we lock eyes and meet for a second on some remote psychic plane and I swear to fucking god he can see into me and through me and he *knows*.

During a long squall of feedback I grab the mic. "What you're hearing right now is only music," I say. "It's just another form of entertainment, like TV or anything else. We're all fucking products," I say, "so get in line and get used to it."

After the show I feel a hand on my shoulder. Ellroy Marx is standing very close to me, his mouth just a few inches from my ear. He nods at the bare stage. "Sweeney, do you really believe all that shit you were saying up there?"

"Ellroy, it's all true," I say, grinning like a madman, so close to him we're almost hugging. "The punks are too late. Coca-Cola and McDonald's already own us. One day we'll wake up with MTV logos tattooed on our heads and IBM computer chips planted in our nuts. Resistance is futile. Now let's go smoke a little grass."

He steps back and eyes me with a mix of amusement and contempt. "Keep it up with that kinda talk, Sweeney, and I'll have you excommunicated."

"From what? The scene? You'd be doing me a favor. You have no thoughts. Or you do but they're a stack of band T-shirts and a column you read in some stupid zine. Why do you have to hold this shit over everyone's head?"

"I don't. I was kidding. Now I'm not. I'll never book any band you're in again."

With that he turns and wanders back through the thinning crowd.

103

I'm alone at a booth in Blake's Diner, picturing the scene as if from the outside looking in, the bright interior fighting the dark downtown Kalamazoo night and the light from in here bleeding out onto the sidewalk. Feels like a kind of lonely poetry in just being in here, the three of us—waitress, cook, customer—like the famous painting.

My mom first took me here long ago, when it was Holly's Grill. Since then it's been Big Al's Falafel, then Holly's Grill again, then Holly's Restaurant, then empty for a long time. Now Blake's Diner, slightly upper-scale but still cheap. Buckwheat pancakes and exotic bottled pops, roasted red pepper sandwiches, that whole scene.

Dirty Donna is the waitress. She always works the overnights. Sort of unfriendly but with an almost-sexy rat's nest of curly brown hair. I picture a tremendous '70s bush down below. And perhaps mild body odor and an arch smile or two after lovemaking. She sits at the counter ignoring me, face buried in *Gravity's Rainbow,* a book she's been reading for a year and a half. I drop my spoon on purpose. She turns. I smile and raise my empty coffee cup. Fuck you, frowner. Free refills. I'll stay all night if I want.

She stands over me with the coffeepot. "Say please."

"Please, Dirty Donna."

"Don't call me that. Were you the jerk that started that?"

"Maybe. What if I was?"

"I'll pour this coffee in your lap."

"Then no, it wasn't me. Sorry."

"Say thanks, jerk."

"Thanks. Oh and could I have another spoon too? I dropped mine."

The cook puts in a new CD, acoustic Bob Dylan. I put my head down on the table. A minute later the door opens and closes. Dirty Donna and the cook are outside smoking. Now it's just me and the music. *It's easy to see without looking too far that not much is really sacred.* I put my head down again and time passes.

There's a tap on the glass to my left. When I look up I see Helene standing out on the sidewalk, still wearing the feather boa and sunglasses. We stare at each other until she goes around the corner and enters the diner.

"Tired?" she says.

"Why?"

"You had your head on the table. You looked asleep."

"I was meditating. What do you want?"

"Can I . . . do you mind if I sit here? Just for a second?"

I am not really ready for this but I gesture at the empty seat. "Be my guest."

"Thanks."

Dirty Donna brings over a glass of water and a menu.

"Where is everyone?" I say.

"I don't know. Home, I guess. I've just been wandering around. I went up to the top of the parking garage for a while. Got kicked out of the Green Top for not being old enough. Took a nap in one of the big chairs at the Radisson till they figured out I wasn't staying there. They gave me the boot and here I am." She takes off the sunglasses.

"Great."

"You guys were really good tonight," she says. "I mean you had your little insanity at the end. But it was . . . I thought it worked this time."

"My little insanity?"

"Yeah. You know. The whole *we're all products* thing."

"You'll get on board sooner or later."

"I'm sure I will."

"Ellroy Marx hates me now. He said he'd never book me again."

"That sounds a little harsh."

"We had another exchange. I shared my views with him privately."

"Whoa. How do you feel about that?"

"Fine," I say. "All true visionaries are hated in their day."

"Now you're just preaching to the choir."

So the old spark returns. Fuck it, I give. I can't fucking figure this chick out. Get that white flag in the air, boys. Dirty Donna comes over with her pad. Helene orders an espresso shake and sweet potato fries. Now and then a car goes by out on South Street.

"I first noticed you in here way down the street."

"Good for you," sipping the last of my coffee.

"And you had your head down and you looked so . . . the whole thing just looked so *sad*. Seeing you here and everything. After everything that happened."

"What do you mean *happened*? Nothing *happened*."

"It did though."

"Really? Where was I?"

"You were right there with me every time. At the party. On

the phone that night you called me." She pauses. "In your bed on the morning of your birthday. You were there. I was the first one to tell you happy eighteenth birthday. I'll remember that forever. Till the day I die. People don't always have to have sex, Vim."

"Tell me about it," I say.

"Or even kiss. Sometimes what happens between two people, it happens here." She touches her head. "And here," she says, touching her heart. The whine of the blender kicks in and we wait it out. We remain silent after it stops and Dirty Donna comes over with the shake and a straw. "More coffee, jerk?"

"Yes, please."

Helene tries sucking the shake through the straw, then gives up and eats a few bites with her spoon. "You have every right to be . . . whatever it is that you are."

"Human. Male."

"Angry."

"No. Not anymore. I'm not angry. I don't know what I am. I know what I *was*. I was everything. I was . . . hate and love and jealousy and fear. Then I disappeared for a while and tried to find peace but all I found was more chaos. And I was guilt and regret and some kind of weird fucked-up nostalgia and sadness for everything ending. And now it's like I said. I don't know. But I know one thing."

"What?"

"I know this thing too is pretty much at an end."

"What thing?" Helene says.

"Whatever this was." I wave a hand between us. "Whatever thing we had. Or didn't have. Whatever went on up here," I say, tapping my head, "it's over."

Helene sits back. Her scars are out in the bright Blake's fluorescence. She touches the boa, rubs the feathers against her cheek. I watch her eyes cloud over and wait, wait for the tears to fall. And they do. They leave pretty tracks down her face.

Dirty Donna brings the fries. Helene looks at them and then at me. There is a strange clarity beaming out from the blueness. "I'm fucked up," she says.

"Why, what are you on?"

"Not like that. You know what I mean. Hearing you talk a second ago, I know you know. There's so many . . . people in our lives, Vim. How do we know how to act around all of them? How do we know who to love? I think about that all the time. And I'm . . . it fucks me up."

I sit there and reflect. Wheeler covered with her suck marks. The darkness and skin of the room in that trailer. The two of them diving down into life. And me in the Fourth Coast with twenty D&D mavens or speeding alone on the highway.

"That may be the first honest thing you've told me."

She shakes her head. "No. I've been honest from the beginning. I'm honest even still. When I saw you that day at Bixby's, when you came into the kitchen, I knew there was gonna be trouble. I could just feel it. And you know what else?"

"What?"

"I wanted there to be trouble. And so did you."

She pours ketchup over the fries. I go downstairs to the bathroom and piss and wash my face. The walls are made of chalkboard and there's a big hunk of chalk. I pick it up and write *So This is Outer Space*. Under that I write *No More Ugly Pussy*. In different handwriting, on another part of the chalkboard, I write *When They Fall at All*.

Back at the table Helene is finishing the fries.

"How's that shake?" I say.

"Good." Her voice pressed out and flat.

"That's it? Just good?"

"It's great," she says. "The best thing I ever tasted."

"Really? Can I try some?"

She pushes it to the center of the table. I hail Dirty Donna and ask for another straw. Helene asks if I'm afraid of her germs. No, it isn't that, I tell her. I put the new straw in and take a sip. It's perfect now, melted just the right amount. "Drink," I say.

We drink. One shake, two straws. Earth angel. The night continues.

OUTSIDE THE AIR IS HEAVY, the streets are empty, the wrought iron clock by Walgreens says ten after ten. But it's said that forever. Really it's approaching two. In four hours Ed'll be rolling out of bed and my mom's alarm will go off and she'll hit snooze and fall asleep, hit snooze and fall asleep. Helene and I walk hand in hand toward Bronson Park. At this hour who cares, there's no one to see. Then into the park, the lush grass and landscaped flower beds sparkling with dew, the monuments to the different wars, the two fountains in the middle, now turned off. Along the north side the Kalamazoo County Building, where my mom and Ed got married.

"So you disappeared," she says. "Besides all the chaos, how was it?"

"Well let's see. I got beat up once. Took in some scenery. Hemingway country up there, don't you know. Played music a lot with my uncle. Ate a lot of doughnuts very late at night. You got my letter, right?"

"Yeah but that wasn't real."

"It was though!"

"You were writing as some character."

"Yeah but the sentiments were real. And the rocks."

"Rocks, what?"

"The pretty little pictured ones. Fuck. Wait a second." My mind flickers back to the sign on the beach. Abigail's warning. "Wait, was the envelope taped?"

"I don't know. I don't remember. Maybe the back of it."

"Those heartless fuckers."

"Who?"

"The Grand Marais postal workers. I drove six fucking hours for that. Seven!"

"You drove seven hours just to get me some rocks?"

"Don't worry. I'll take back the ones I gave to my mom."

"Vim, don't you dare."

She takes off her All-Stars and walks along in the wet grass and tells me how good it feels, the cool wet grass between her toes. I'm thinking of her mother and the diamonds. She takes my hand again. I feel the full weight and joy of life as we walk. The white hum of the night is heavy with it. There is an ease between us, no more trouble, an absence of history, ours or the world's. The sun will rise but not till the morning. Life will continue but not till I want it to.

We walk on and stop by the fountain with the metal sculptures of children sitting or in action poses on long concrete rectangles rising out of the water. Helene steps in. She sloshes out to the middle and stands before one of them. Stares deeply into the blank eyes. "I know the guy who modeled for this one," she says. "He was a friend of my cousin's. Or he was a long time ago."

"Wow. I've been seeing his face all my life. Whatever happened to him?"

"I don't know but if I had to just make something up, let's see. I'd say he lives in a not so great part of Cleveland with his wife and baby, a girl, and he's the manager at Builder's Square."

"That's depressing."

"Not to him it isn't. It's my fantasy and that's the life he wanted. Why don't you come on in here. The water's perfect."

"I don't know. It looks kinda slimy."

"It is, for sure. But you're not scared of a little slime, are you?"

She could almost be a sculpture herself, out there with her little band of lost boys and girls, frozen, forever young, like her cousin's friend. Maybe he's in Cleveland or maybe he's dead. Even if he is, he'll never *really* die. Isn't that the goal in the end? Yes. Not to be famous necessarily but to at least leave a trace. Vim Sweeney was here. 1974 to whenever. He was a part of this world, he existed and was loved by at least one person. *Yeah but what if that person's a mute drooling maniac?* Doesn't matter. There was love. He felt it and gave back as much as he could.

One day you'll stop breathing too.

I step into the water with my shoes and socks on, walking over the pennies, nickels and dimes of all of Kalamazoo's wishers and dreamers. I've thrown change in here myself. My mom would drag me to the Kalamazoo art fair and while she was off looking at hand-thrown pottery I'd circle the fountain and maybe throw in a penny or two. Where are my wishes? Have any of them come true?

Now I'm out by Helene and I take both of her hands. There's a split-second blast of bass from a car passing over on

Park Street and then just the sound of water lapping around our ankles. "What happens now?" she says.

Some stars in the sky, some satellites. "It's gonna be okay," I say, "but just tell me," my hands now touching the feathers around her neck and also, very gently, the skin beneath, "just tell me if you mind that I'm doing this."

"No," she says, "I don't mind at all."

"No please don't say another word don't I'm just going to," as my hand runs upward along her neck to her cheek. She opens her mouth and takes a breath to speak and I say, "No please not a word." But she is whispering again words I can't hear.

My heart pounds a Bo Diddley beat. *Dum-da-dum-da-dum-da-dum-dum.* And when we kiss, this city, this almost-city recedes in flame and the sun's ghost becomes our breath. I have waited so long and wanted it so bad and I'll die remembering the taste. Coffee ice cream and Blistex lip stuff. I pull her closer. She pulls me back. Her hands reach and grab. She bites my bottom lip, sucks it into her mouth. Then the top. The feathers tickle my chin. We are all hands and lips and when finally it ends I want to fall to my knees in the water and beg and scream, not for another kiss but for life to always be like this, bursting open, feeling every second with an atom-smashing heart.

Truth is love is change.

104

Dear god please fill me with the light of something larger than myself amen.

105

I drove down 37th Street across M-89 around Gull Lake on a cool overcast day, more like mid-November, and the run-down houses around the bay looked small and weird and gave way to the mansions set back in the trees, down long driveways, away from the road. When I got back Ed was out at the brand-new Grillmaster standing looking through strands of thin gray smoke blown here and there and when he saw me pull in he raised the spatula and nodded hello. Suddenly the rage went out of my head like a dream down the shower drain and I knew who I was a little bit. I didn't get out of the car right away. Instead I sat there a long time staring, hands at ten and two, looking out through the windshield back at Ed Hoekstra, my true father.

106

The moonlight spills through the trees. The starlight, the satellites, the blank heavens. The road. The peace way deep in the shadows and earth. The steel mist hovering over the water. The dark houses and dreams inside, in the rooms in sleeping minds. The left-on televisions and frantic blue beamed out at no one. The driveways, the lawns. The comfort of solitude and the courage to awaken again and go forth. The awareness of absence, reaching out to touch a hand that's not there. The ache.

107

I wish I could show you, I wish you could see, I wish I was a screen at the East-Towne. Helene, your stare from out in the seats would fill me up with your longings, the pretty things you see when you close your eyes and the bad things too. Because you can't have light without its opposite. The dreams you have for your own life and the lives of your mother and brother too. Even your father out roaming the void.

Your name still echoes.

Helene. Helene.

Sometimes I say it out loud and no one hears except the fireflies.

You are the truth and I am a lie. I hide my pain and yours is in the world under the bright lights and you are unashamed. Give me a sweater made from your smell and whispers.

108

"Love happens," my mother says, "just like shit. I thought I'd be with Joe Sweeney forever. I really did. I believed it. My parents loved him. I loved him. I thought I did anyway. No I'm sure I did but who knows. I was what. I was twenty-eight. That was a while ago now. And I'll tell you something. Afterward, after he was gone for good and it was just you and me and we were all set up in our one-bedroom in Jackson. After it was over I felt like I'd failed at something very important. Love. I felt like a failure. It took me a long time to feel anything else."

We are at the Bayview. Bro's band is in town. Says on the sign *DREAM POLICE ALL WEEKEND ENJOY OUR RIBS BEST AROUND*. Apparently they've done away with their wisdom nuggets. I think of the Titties of Invention and smile.

"What?" my mom says, smiling too.

"Nothing," I say. "Mom, listen." I move my empty glass around in a figure eight on the table. "I'm sorry about all that. What you just told me. It sounds bad."

"Well it was. But it's nothing to be sorry about now. Besides.

I wasn't really alone. I *thought* I was, sure. I remember one after-noon, sitting on the edge of the bed, numb and staring. I thought *This is it. Now I'm done. Washed up at thirty-two. Alone forever.* Then I heard you in the next room crying. What could I do? I got up and tried to get on with life. I had a baby. You. And then, you know, slowly things got better."

It's still early in the set and the Dream Police are playing the mellower tunes for the oldsters. "Margaritaville." "Under the Boardwalk." And the one that just ended that goes *Give me the beat boy to free my soul I wanna get lost in your rock and roll and drift away.* Bro looks out from the stage after tuning his Strat and we exchange nods. Cherie is not here. I wish she'd driven down. Bro's supposed to stay at our house tonight but who knows where he might end up? It's hard to free yourself from your own history.

He does a solo harmonic intro high up on the neck, then the whole band breaks into "Sleepwalk," the classic fifties love-song chords, C, Am, F, G, and it hits me again, like it does every time, that beautiful thing, music digging in, making me whole.

"You wanna dance?" my mom says.

"Do I wanna *what*?"

"Come on," she says, pushing her seat back, holding out a hand.

"Mom, please." I look around, trying to see who's seeing this.

"Vim, come on. Enough," she says.

I hesitate for only one more second before I take her hand and let her lead me out to the dance floor. We do the box step, slowly shuffling back and forth. I feel a strange peace wash over me and I become perfectly calm, as if everything I ever loved

Grab On to Me Tightly as if I Knew the Way

was here in this room. I see our waitress filling a drink tray over at the bar, all the people around us dancing, in love, never wanting it to end, my uncle playing guitar, making it weep, his fingers burning under the cheap red lights. I see all this as I dance with my mother.

109

Dad,

All this time all these years and so much anger. Sometimes feels like I walk around and it's always there under the surface burning under the skin ready to come out. And what do I say to you now? I read your letter and hated you more. Why? Why when I sometimes want to forgive you so desperately and know the only way I'll ever be free is to let go of all these awful things I hold on to, almost cling to. Sometimes I think all I want in the world is to be able to forgive you, to learn how to love you. But always that part of me shuts off like a light switch.

Why is it so impossible to let go?

This is the hardest thing I've ever done. I can barely look at the page but my hand keeps moving because if I don't tell you now I'll never tell you and if I don't send this tomorrow I'll never send it and we'll live on like this, never diving down into the heart of things. And what can it mean to be your son anyway when I already have a father, the man who saved me, and you don't even know him, you only know his name.

I remember your wedding, actually after the wedding, the night before I was going to fly home. I couldn't sleep and suddenly had this terrible fear of flying and every time I shut my eyes I saw myself on a plane exploding in midair and it was so bad my arms and legs felt like not even a part of me and I couldn't take a breath. So I got up and went downstairs trying to be so quiet. I took soft steps on the stairs and stopped whenever the wood creaked. But you were already there sitting at the table and the only light came from the little night-light far away in the kitchen behind you. You didn't hear me come down and I stood on the last step and watched. You were just sitting there like you were just thinking. Then you looked up and saw me and said my name. You turned on a small lamp and I sat down too. Seemed like silence for a long time. It was the first time I saw you had green eyes like mine when all the time before I'd thought I'd gotten green eyes from my uncle, first time I saw that you were maybe at one time handsome.

You asked what was wrong and I told you. I said I was certain that tomorrow on the plane I would die. I felt like as sure as we were sitting there talking that by that time the next night I'd be gone, dropped out of the sky to the burning earth and you laughed quietly but there wasn't meanness in it and you told me all the things they tell you about flying being safer than driving and you're more likely to crash your car on the way to the airport etc. etc. You said my name again then, put your hand over mine on the table and it felt so weird being touched by you I almost pulled my hand away and you said: You're not going to die, you're going to be fine, and you patted my hand and maybe sensed the strangeness because you pulled away and I remember the lamp cast light on your arms and shirt but your face was a shadow with a dull halo glowing behind it from the light in the kitchen. I remember thinking I'd die on the plane never having known you and did I even care and if you had asked me that night I would have said no, would have said no a month ago, but it should be obvious now that I care but don't have the slightest fucking clue what to do about it and you know you were only half right that night. You said I wasn't going to die and I didn't and you also said I'd be fine and I wasn't.

I remember the next thing I said after your airplane speech. I asked if you believed in God. It was one of those things I asked before I knew I was thinking it and you looked at me curiously and there was distance in your eyes and you didn't say a word, only shook your head slowly back and forth no and I wonder sometimes if that's still your answer, that slow no, the same way I wonder what was running through your mind as you stood looking down at me in my crib when I was just a baby and you knew you had to leave and you knew if what you said in your letter was true you knew you had to leave to save me because you saw yourself becoming your own distant father and you were throwing me back to the place where I came from my mother and you knew the world and you knew you wanted me in it alone and you could not help me, you could not show me, you could not teach me anything and you let another man teach me, a man I know and love in ways I could never

know or love you. When the anger takes hold of me I think
if you were here before me and I had one more shot at you I
would lunge and swing out and bite through your neck to
the veins and muscle and scream into your blood: You were
only a coward I was only a baby she was only my mother
don't give up on me now like you did back then, please, fuck
you, I'm trying, it's killing me to care but who knows, ten,
twenty, a thousand years from now you might make sense to
me. And maybe then I'll make sense to you.

110

Hot night, black water, high silver clouds. We're out on Gull
Lake, flying over its surface at dangerous speeds, hair whipping
and crazy, blown back into helmets. Jake and I and Stevens Mc-
Neil. McNeil's dad's a dermatologist and their boat is *Skin Deep*.
McNeil gunning it. Jake's arms in the air as if he's on a roller
coaster. Only the roar of the motor out here, and the wind, so
it's easy to forget all the great hurts and minor victories. Just let
the night be yours and breathe.

There are other stern lights all across the lake, little green
stars traveling over the void. Pretty soon a few boats are tied
together and there's a good old boat party going, everyone
hopping, beer in hand, from boat to boat, cigarette ends glowing orange. All the stereos play different music. Bob Marley.
Jane's Addiction. CCR. I get McNeil to put in the Replace-

ments' *Let It Be,* a good party album, life and death, the full spectrum.

There seem to be a lot of new faces or maybe only shadows obscuring the old ones and I can't tell the difference. The girls I see have long pretty legs and long damp hair and wet T-shirts clinging to the tits and bikinis beneath. They smell like washed-away perfume and suntan lotion and powder-fresh deodorant and shampoo. Every lovely mouth shooting smoke at the sky. Oh world, oh life, I'm yours to keep.

Jake hands me a cold Miller High Life and we drink.

"It's gonna be weird but we'll do it," he says. "We'll get another drummer and play. The Judy Lumpers cannot be done."

"Yes they can."

"Then we'll think of a new name too. Doesn't matter as long as we don't give up. We still have a lot of music left to play together, you and I."

"Yeah? Will we ever make anything good?"

"We'll make something shitty. Who cares? I like our stuff now, some of it. But we can make all the bad music we want till we plow on through and get to the good. Get to the better. There's plenty of time for all of it, Vim."

I take a long drink and listen to Paul Westerberg singing in his ravaged voice *look me in the eyes and tell me that I'm satisfied.*

"Tell me something," Jake says. "I wanna know."

"What?"

"Was it worth it, all this, for the one kiss?"

There are people in the water now. I watch them dive through the air, down into nothing, and surface a few seconds later, laughing, wiping their eyes. Distant boats speed on by and their wakes finally reach us. *Skin Deep* rocks gently.

The answer is a whisper. *"Yes."*

A gauzy liquid sliver of moon. Heat lightning flashing almost sideways over the fields and flat country just north of the lake. Ghostly bodies move through the black ink water. Along the shore the big houses twinkling, the money. I get up and switch boats.

Different voices, another frosty High Life, a girl's laughter and her hand on my wrist, the fingers slender and warm. Come to me some morning before dawn and touch me with them, hold me. Her arms smooth except for the goose bumps.

A soft pink bubble glows in the southwesterly sky.

The lights of Kalamazoo.

I take off my shirt, shoes and socks and stand in the glow of the stern light, arms out, just waiting, breathing, nothing more. Sometimes that's the only joy. And the joy to be had in that one great leap. When I hit water the world and all I know vanishes. I sink down a ways in the endless darkness then kick up fast and resurface.

ACKNOWLEDGMENTS

I'm hugely grateful to PJ Mark and John Williams for believing in me and in this book and coming out of nowhere when I was feeling down to make the only dream I ever had come true; to Tom Beller for encouragement, friendship, and support; Jay Ryan for the amazing cover; and SM for supplying the title and making the music. Thanks also to Farrin Jacobs, Irini Spanidou, Jonathan Baumbach, Michael Cunningham, *Open City*, Betsy Crane Brandt, Jill Jakes, Megan Robinson, Saïd Sayrafiezadeh, Scott Smith, Greg Purcell, Uncle Barry, Dan Buettner, Mark Weston, Jean Tittle, and Mike Charles. Special thanks and love to Paul Bayer, Trish Chappell, Erin Dwight, Stephen Lynch, and Debora Vilas Boas. I'd also like to give a shout-out to the city of Kalamazoo, Michigan, whose general vibe and musical and literary underground during the years that I lived there helped define me.

P.S.

Insights,
Interviews
& More . . .

A Conversation with Bryan Charles

Debora Vilas Boas

We'll begin by pulling an abrupt **Booknotes** *stunt: Where was Bryan Charles born?*

I was born in Troy, Michigan, in 1974.

Where were you raised? What events from your childhood stand out?

I lived in Kalamazoo until I was nine, then moved to a very small town about twenty minutes away called Galesburg. It wasn't suburban . . . more of a country scene with a lot of woods and the houses far apart and no brothers or sisters—it was a lonely only-child kind of existence. My memories of childhood involve hanging out either by myself or with this neighbor kid who lived across the street. Eventually he started going to a Christian school and we lost touch. There was a lot of bike riding and exploring, and early on I got heavily into music. I remember going to Meijer's, this big regional superstore before such things were so pervasive, and spending my allowance on tapes; I think the first few I bought were the *Footloose* soundtrack, *Strip*

> ❝ Galesburg wasn't suburban . . . more of a country scene with a lot of woods and the houses far apart and no brothers or sisters—it was a lonely only-child kind of existence. ❞

by Adam Ant, and *Thriller*—that kind of stuff. We got cable, and like a lot of people my age I spent a lot of time watching early MTV. I was really enthralled with all the imagery from those videos cycling around in my head. When I think back there were no big events . . . more like a series of moments that ended up being life-altering in little ways: waiting for songs like "Our House" to come on the radio so I could tape them; going to the Richland Roller Rink—fairly typical mid-eighties childhood stuff that now seems like something from the fifties to me, a bygone era, a totally different, more innocent age.

What did your parents do?

My stepfather, now retired, worked in a paper mill all his life. The paper industry was big in southwest Michigan, and there were several large paper mills, all closed now. Like a lot of the manufacturing jobs, they disappeared. My mom started out as a journalist working around the Detroit area, then got into communications as an editor for a hospital newsletter, and later started her own business.

When and how did you first take to writing?

The first thing I wrote was a poem in fourth grade called "Underneath." It was a grim piece of verse about how the world was being overrun with wars and dying. My mom still has a photocopy. I kept writing poems and started reading books way beyond my comprehension—*A Clockwork Orange*, *Slaughterhouse-Five* and *The Sun Also Rises*— just because they were around, downstairs on the bookshelf. My first real experiments with prose came in seventh grade. Since ▶

A Conversation with Bryan Charles
(continued)

Less Than Zero had come out as a movie and I'd read the book they were grim Bret Easton Ellis imitation pieces, stark and with a lot of drugs, which of course I hadn't done and knew nothing about. And then I guess it was just an evolution from there, throughout high school and college and beyond, always reading, writing, and imitating. But it started with poetry, which now that I really think about it, strikes me as meaningful—always going for the beautiful line, the stunner, fucking around with context and associations.

Have you any unusual or otherwise compelling anecdotes about your collegiate experience?

During college (I went to Western Michigan University) I lived in this big house with a bunch of other like-minded weirdos. We had two three-bedroom apartments but it was really like one big house, a communal thing. There were instruments everywhere and people were always playing or listening to music. In my apartment there was a typewriter on the table and so there was always writing too, the whole table covered with pages of free associations and poetry and little prose pieces and humor pieces. It was the most unself-consciously creative time of my life: just writing for the sheer joy, playing music for the sheer joy, no competition, no real knowledge of or interest in the big business creative arts industries or what was happening on the coasts, just holed away in Kalamazoo doing my thing. I didn't know it then but it's what they call "finding your

> 66 My first real experiments with prose came in seventh grade—grim Bret Easton Ellis imitation pieces, stark and with a lot of drugs. 99

voice." I took all the writing workshops, had a lot of dysfunctional make-out sessions, and did tiny tours with my band. I don't know how compelling this is but I really do long for that old mind-set, wish I could unlearn certain things. Raymond Chandler said everything a writer learns about the craft of fiction takes just a little bit away from his need to write at all, and I agree with that to an extent. I don't want to sound like a washed-up football player whose glory days were when he was nineteen, but the hardest thing for me as I go along and learn more about how to write and what it really takes to be good is holding on to that sense of fun and wonder that I had sitting at the table at 909 Walwood and just putting a piece of paper in the typewriter and letting it fly.

Name some peculiar jobs you've had.

Summers during college I worked in the same paper mill as my stepdad. I worked the swing shift, which meant that a few weeks into the summer I didn't know if I was awake or asleep. I was what they call a sixth hand on the paper machine. It was a lot of grunt work, spraying ankle-deep paper pulp off the basement floor with rats and roaches everywhere at three in the morning, and crawling into the machine on "down days" with a metal scraper and scraping crust off the conveyor. The good thing was, when the machine was running well I was on my own and I'd usually have a book with me or go and bury myself in a "broke box," a big wooden bin filled with paper scraps, and take a fifteen- or twenty- ▶

> 66 I took all the writing workshops, had a lot of dysfunctional make-out sessions, and did tiny tours with my band. 99

minute nap. By the end of the summer I looked like I'd aged five years from lack of sleep and eating Hostess fruit pies, again at three or four in the morning. Just after college, the year before I moved to New York, I worked as a substitute teacher. I taught all grades at first and then took over a high school sociology class. It was only supposed to be for six weeks but it ended up being an entire semester. I was twenty-three, didn't know how to write a lesson plan, didn't know anything, and I was on my own. It was more exhausting than the paper mill and gave me a whole new respect for teachers. It's really hard work with little reward. Most of my students were juniors and seniors, which meant they weren't much younger than me, so there was some strange tension there: do I talk to these kids like we're all just hanging out, do I try to be stern, or what? I even did parent-teacher conferences—flannel shirt untucked, Beatle haircut—though I don't think I was very reassuring to the parents. I was so filled with anxiety about my own future that I think it translated to a lot of weirdness trying to help other young people define theirs. After I moved to New York it was all just office jobs and things were very, very dull until 9/11; then there were a couple of years of frantic life-living and now a dull office again.

What is your earliest memory of reading and being influenced by a book?

I have a couple early memories of reading. I remember *Alexander and the Terrible, Horrible, No Good, Very Bad Day,* which was

> 66 Summers during college I worked the swing shift in a paper mill. By the end of the summer I looked like I'd aged five years from lack of sleep and eating Hostess fruit pies. 99

my favorite book when I was a kid, and also *Where the Sidewalk Ends* by Shel Silverstein, which I read over and over. My first real immersion in a book that just had a huge influence on me (notwithstanding my Ellis imitations) was *Jesus' Son* by Denis Johnson. I had a fiction workshop in the fall of 1993 and the book was just out in paperback. My teacher brought it to class and read a couple of the shorter stories aloud. Afterward I asked to look at it and I just felt this strange pull. I bought a copy and went totally nuts for those stories. I loved the poetry—it was exactly the kind of thing I was (and am) going for in my writing. When I found out Johnson is also a poet I got the book with his collected poems and read everything else by him. I bought *Already Dead* the day it came out, the same with *The Name of the World*. I can still quote long passages from *Jesus' Son*, and I told my editor John Williams that signing on with Harper was like a guy who really worships Nirvana getting signed to Geffen (Records), on account of the Denis Johnson connection.

Do you have any writerly quirks? When and where do you write? PC or pen?

I don't have too many writerly quirks. I live in a railroad apartment and the back room is my writing room. When I was working on my book I got up every day at seven and started "preparing": getting into the mind-set, pacing, turning off Howard Stern and then turning it on again. I have an old G3 PowerBook, but I'm looking to eliminate the distractions that go with a computer— ▶

> 66 My first real immersion in a book that just had a huge influence on me was *Jesus' Son* by Denis Johnson. 99

e-mail, Internet, etc. I bought an old IBM Selectric, which is also useful because it renders immediate rewriting impossible (or at least more cumbersome). I guess a quirk of mine would be constant and immediate rewriting, writing a sentence then instantly reworking it. I don't think that's healthy. I have a whole folder full of handwritten notes for my next book, enough material at this point for at least the first quarter, so that's different. Lately I've been feeling pretty burned out on hypermodern methods of composition and communication.

> 66 I bought an old IBM Selectric, which is also useful because it renders immediate rewriting impossible (or at least more cumbersome). 99

What do you rely upon for stimulation? Do you observe any particular beverage ritual?

Coffee is the big stimulant. Over the years, especially the jobless book-writing years, I've eaten obscene amounts of peanut butter. I'm sure that if all the peanut butter I've eaten appeared before me in mountain form I'd be really disgusted with myself. I've cut back, though. A peanut butter and banana sandwich, the old standby, has little appeal these days.

What interests or enthusiasms do you have (e.g., hobbies, outdoor pursuits)?

The only things besides writing that I really love to do are listening to and playing music. I still have a big vinyl collection and lots of CDs, and I spend a lot of time just sitting on the floor listening to records. I used to buy new music all the time, new seven-inches by bands I didn't know, scour the used bins for gems. I don't really have the energy for that anymore but once in a while I still get obsessed with a new band. I also like to walk a lot. I take long walks every day, partly out of necessity since I live roughly a mile from the most convenient subway, but taking the train into Manhattan for a Whitman-style perambulation is still one of my favorite things to do.

Wife, partner, children, pet(s)?

No wife, no pets. But a lot of my friends are living that dream: marriage with a couple of dogs, home ownership, even a baby or two here and there. I'm content to view that scene from a distance at this point. Then again, I don't want to be a forty-four-year-old urban bachelor dude hitting on young chicks in a workshop or something, telling them they really should read Don DeLillo.

> " I don't want to be a forty-four-year-old urban bachelor dude hitting on young chicks in a workshop or something, telling them they really should read Don DeLillo. "

Writing *Grab On to Me Tightly* . . .

I SPENT THE SUMMER OF 2001 sitting in a cubicle high up in the World Trade Center writing mutual fund brochures for a global financial powerhouse that I felt pretty certain couldn't care less whether I lived, died, or pissed in the wind. I was making $54,000 a year at the time, an outrageous sum to my 26-year-old mind, both in terms of its relation to the actual amount of work I did and the future I'd envisioned for myself in my undergrad days. I was an English major, after all, and had taken every conceivable combination of writing workshops without once giving a thought to the kind of job I might land. My grasp of money and its consequences was so poor that I entrusted my mother with my student loan forms and took a fifth year basically just for the fuck of it. A year and a half after graduation I moved from Michigan to New York with $1,500, believing it to be a good bit of money. It was not. But luckily the economy and job market were stellar, mutual funds were hot shit, and if one could string words into near-meaningless banalities one was guaranteed at least a few rounds of interviews on the financial writing scene.

At the time that I began my corporate adventures I had not read a word of Richard Yates. Yet my head swam with the kind of delusions and rationalizations that afflict so many of his white-collar worker drone characters, the most famous of which is *Revolutionary Road*'s Frank Wheeler. *This is only a temporary thing. It's such good money and you can write on the weekends. You work for a big corporation but there's a devilish irony at play here too because you used to be in punk bands and insert a caustic edge into even your most innocuous-seeming office banter and you're really in the end only an imposter collecting a paycheck and not a real actual corporate dude so ha!*

This type of thinking can carry you for a while—even a whole lifetime—especially if the boat is not rocked, and by that summer I'd worn myself quite a groove: spend six or eight weekends grinding out a short story, send it out to all the little magazines, suppress if possible the faint flickers of hope, then file away the rejections as they came in one or three or eight months later. I wouldn't exactly say I was depressed during that time, but if Fitzgerald was correct in his assessment that the test of a first-rate intelligence is the ability to hold two opposed ideas in the mind at the same time and still retain the ability to function, then it was a test I was failing and a kind of minor-league crack-up had certainly begun. I worried endlessly that I was not writing enough and that what I did write would never be published; I kept constant tabs on my few writer friends, despairing at their various successes; I greedily devoured every hot book of the moment, staring at the photo of the invariably young and attractive person on the back cover, wondering what mysterious thing they possessed that I did not. Meanwhile, I had all the money I needed, at least for my solitary renter's life, as well as top-tier health insurance and 401(k) programs. It was a rather joyless existence, all discipline, perseverance, and deferred contentment, which was perfectly in keeping with my only slightly warped view of the way a real writer should exist.

Now it all seems like such a very long time ago.

At some point in the fall of 1998, when I was new to the city and sending out résumés though not yet employed, I pulled a large floor speaker up to my roommate's computer (there was then no chair in the apartment) and wrote a very short story about an encounter I'd had six years earlier, the memory of which I could not shake. It was about a time one very hot day in the summer of 1992 when I met a girl with scars on her arms who was reading *Naked Lunch.* It was her bible, she said. We talked for maybe ten minutes. And that was it, that was the end of our interaction. In the ineffable way of memory, though, I kept envisioning the scene, and the original players, two real people, ceased to be real. New words bubbled up, dimly at first, and their conversation seemed to be one I was accidentally overhearing rather than one I was piecing together over a period of years. The story I wrote was six pages long. I called it "Scars," sent it out some number of times, and no one ever published it. But I ▶

thought of it regularly, and as time passed the voices of those two young characters grew louder in my head. Their histories became clearer and I saw them in different situations, moving and speaking and laughing. In August 2001, a few weeks before I started grad school, I returned to them and in a single sitting expanded the story from six to twenty pages. New characters stepped out of the ether and the writing, as it is on only rare and therefore very happy days, was effortless. I called the story "My Hideous Bride" after a song written by the main character, whose name was now Vim Sweeney. I felt even then that it represented a turning point for me as a writer, a loosening, a freeing. So when the first fiction workshop of my MFA career assembled in the final week of August and my teacher Irini Spanidou asked who would like to be the first up to bat, mine was the only hand that shot up.

The critique went down a week later and I remember only that I was insanely nervous, shaking almost. Irini said in her closing comments that she was interested in the voice and characters of the story and had it ever occurred to me to try and break the thing open, write a little longer, see what might happen, and maybe make it into a, well, a novel? The answer was no. It was all I could do working forty hours a week to put together 6,000 words, but I think I equivocated and hinted that, yes, writing a novel about these people had been my intention all along. I went out into the night feeling I don't know what. Fall was coming, my favorite time of year, and I'd written a pretty good story. My classmates and teacher took me seriously as a writer and shit, allow me just a sliver of optimism here because the worm might really be turning for me and. . . .

The following Tuesday I went to work and a hijacked plane crashed into the building next to the one in which I was sitting. A short time later my building was hit. By ten thirty that morning, of course, neither building existed. I stayed away for two weeks, first in New Jersey and then in Michigan, until implicit pressures became explicit and I was urged back to work by people above me with a greater interest in the fate of the company than I'd been able to muster in even my brightest moods. And my mood in the period following September 11 was by no means bright.

This is not the time or the place to go into all that I was feeling back then. It should suffice for now to admit that the next couple of years were the worst of my life. Yet they were also the best in a way (and it took almost until this second to arrive at that conclusion), because I was tapped in to something rare, an overwhelming sense of what truly mattered and what

I really wanted from life. On the evening of October 20, 2001, I sat down in this very room and started writing the book you now hold in your hands using "My Hideous Bride" as a starting point. I lasted three more months at the job and then quit and threw everything into the novel. I wrote every day. When I wasn't writing or at school talking about writing I was out walking aimlessly, listening to the sounds of the city and my life savings blowing away in the wind, and thinking about my book and the people in it and what was going to happen to them and how I could make it better and would I ever finish it and even if I did would it ever be published and even if it was would anyone anywhere ever give two shits?

That last question is obviously one I can't answer. Everything that happens next is beyond my control. Writing *Grab On to Me Tightly As If I Knew the Way* both drove me insane and kept me from breaking apart entirely. And as I contemplate its origins in the final lap of another summer, far removed from the one in the book yet still in view of the one that came before times got bad, I am grateful for its existence in the physical sense as a thing you can put on your shelf, but also as an intangible force that gave back everything I put into it and more.

July 24, 2005

Author's Picks

I PREVIOUSLY MENTIONED a story I wrote called "My Hideous Bride" that I felt represented a departure point for me as a writer. Well, that story was written under the influence of *Airships,* by Barry Hannah, which I'd picked up almost randomly at a used bookstore. It was exactly the kind of writing I was searching for. The stories weren't polished little MFA gems with some dude staring through a window at dusk having an epiphany at the end. They were brutal and beautiful and funny and poetic and they screamed off the page and into my nerve centers. My book also owes a debt to his short novel *Ray,* which turned me on to the narrative possibilities of fragmentation and rearrangement (B. R. Myers will probably give me poor marks but what the hell). And if you think Hannah did his best work in the Lish-ruled seventies, I encourage you to pick up *Yonder Stands Your Orphan,* his most recent and best book.

Richard Fariña's *Been Down So Long It Looks Like Up to Me* has an introduction by Thomas Pynchon and so hardly needs a push from me, but it was recommended at a critical time. In addition to title echoes my book contains a fairly direct nod to Gnossos and his crew.

Another writer who needs no further endorsement to keep moving units is F. Scott Fitzgerald. If you've only ever read *The Great Gatsby,* though, I recommend *Tender is the Night.* If you're feeling really ambitious, reading *F. Scott Fitzgerald: A Life in Letters* cover to cover is almost as good as a grad school education.

The Quick and the Dead, by Joy Williams, is a wonderful, weirdly overlooked masterpiece

> 66 The stories in *Airships,* by Barry Hannah, were brutal and beautiful and funny and poetic and they screamed off the page and into my nerve centers. 99

and another book I happened to read just as I was getting my act together on the novel. I picked it up again and again, and rereading certain passages helped me stay focused on the concept of writing as an art that can blow people's minds.

Richard Yates cornered the market on cubicle malaise, but with the Grimes sisters in *The Easter Parade* he proved he's equally adept at chronicling the ruinous effects divorce has on children. His book *A Good School* falls on the pitch-black end of the coming-of-age spectrum.

Much brighter though still in that ballpark is Tobias Wolff's *Old School*, whose prep school writing contests reflect larger truths about the desire to create. And Wolff, it must be said, wrote one of the greatest coming-of-age books ever, his memoir *This Boy's Life*.

Finally, I recommend the lyric sheet to Pavement's *Brighten the Corners*. The album is musically close to flawless, but even if late-nineties indie rock isn't your thing the words alone are worth the price of admission. Especially with "Shady Lane," "Starlings of the Slipstream," and "Type Slowly," Stephen Malkmus achieves pure poetry.

SOUNDTRACK: BEST OF THE NINETIES

I had planned to write a whole thing about the music in the book, but most of the name-checked bands have been written about ad nauseam (how many times must one hear that *Nevermind* was an epochal album?). Besides, the trend of young fiction writers venturing into a kind of nostalgia-drenched music noncriticism is one that vaguely irritates me. At the same time, I can't resist throwing my hat in the ring and as a compromise would like to mention a few old favorites not typically found on those ubiquitous best of the nineties lists.

The Laughing Hyenas, *Life of Crime* (1990)

It's hard to believe that the man who recorded this went on to produce *Nevermind* and *Siamese Dream,* two slick-sounding albums that are now essential classic rock. This is dark Midwestern Stooges rock that even now couldn't get played on modern rock radio. John Brannon's vocals would scare too many people.

Rollinghead, *Daddyhorse* (1992)

This is a Kalamazoo band, and unless you were there or know someone who was you probably won't find their CDs, which is a shame. Dave Grant, the frontman, is without a doubt one of the most gifted ▶

Author's Picks *(continued)*

singer/songwriters I ever heard. He has a perfect, timeless rock and roll voice and his lyrics on this record still give me shivers. I find the fact that this band didn't blow up in the insane post-*Nevermind* climate that brought global fame to Candlebox a moral outrage.

Jawbreaker, *24 Hour Revenge Therapy* (1994)

Back when I followed such things I predicted that Jawbreaker, not Green Day, would bring punk to the masses. The band instead imploded one album later and Green Day, strangely, is bigger than ever. At least The Offspring aren't famous anymore.

Superchunk, *Here's Where the Strings Come In* (1995)

This band is still around and still making good music, but one of the problems with longevity in rock is that it tends to dull the shine of a band's more brilliant moments (I might be more compelled to revisit *The Joshua Tree,* for instance, if U2 had stopped making music after *Achtung Baby).* This record is loud and fun and deep and its ferocity still blows my mind.

Girls Against Boys, *House of GVSB* (1996)

For a few years in the mid-nineties this band was as hot as the sun and everyone I knew bought their records. The love crested with *House*—a moody, sexy album so self-assured that it seemed like the band was going to take over the world—and then faded entirely two years later with their turdish major-label debut.

D on't miss the next book by your favorite author. Sign up now for AuthorTracker by visiting www.AuthorTracker.com.

The Monorchid, *Let Them Eat the Monorchid* (1997)

In the weird days just after college, when I was a substitute teacher and totally confused, I would get drunk by myself on Friday nights and listen to this. I'd be so tired from getting up at six and suffering the abuses of teenagers all day that I'd pass out around 9:30 with the songs from this record floating around my brain like demented lullabies. ⌒